Where the Universes Converge

a BALKY POINT ADVENTURES
companion book

Copyright © 2023 Pam Stucky

Published in the United States by Wishing Rock Press.

ISBN-13: 978-1-940800-33-2 (print)
ISBN-13: 978-1-940800-32-5 (ebook)

wishingrockpress.com

CHOOSE YOUR OWN UNIVERSE

Where the Universes Converge

a BALKY POINT ADVENTURES
companion book

PAM STUCKY

Wishing Rock Press

The Balky Point Adventures

The Universes Inside the Lighthouse
The Secret of the Dark Galaxy Stone
The Planet of the Memory Thieves
The Perils of the Infinite Task

The Balky Point Adventures
Choose Your Own Universe companion books

The Ghost Planet
Where the Universes Converge

pamstucky.com

WARNING!

Do NOT read this book straight through from beginning to end!

There are people who believe that every time we make a choice, a new, parallel universe is formed. In this universe, our lives continue with the choice we made. In the newly formed universe, our path follows the choices we didn't take here.

This is no ordinary book.

Here, you can experience all those universes.

Here, you can discover where your different choices might have led.

In this book, YOU are the main character. Just as in real life, YOU make the choices. And YOU face the consequences.

At the end of each section you'll be given a choice. Think over your options, then turn to the designated page or click on the appropriate link.

Every choice will take you down a different path.

Some choices lead to happiness and adventure.

Some choices may lead to your demise.

Choose carefully.

And when you reach the end of a path, return to the start and do it all again!

Note that the Choose Your Own Universe stories are companion books to the Balky Point Adventure novels. Each Choose Your Own Universe story stands alone and can be read by itself or alongside the others. To help you, the reader, understand how this group of adventurers came together, the opening backstory is the same for each Choose Your Own Universe book. But after that, what happens next is up to you!

THE BACKSTORY

The sound of waves crashing against the island shore echoes up from the cliffs below and there's a slight ocean spray in the air. It's sunny and tranquil. Today will be just another uneventful vacation day, you think to yourself.

This morning you decided to meander a path near the cabin your family has rented for vacation, to see where it might take you, and the trail has ended here.

Before you is a lighthouse with a tower reaching into the sky, and a short building nestled at its base. Giant red and white stripes encircle the tower. You can see a long set of stairs next to the building, leading down to the beach below. The stairs are tempting, but you want to see what's inside the lighthouse first.

As you head toward the building, a small rock in your path catches your eye. It is gray, with a solid white stripe wrapping around the entire rock. Your grandma once pointed out a similar stone to you, telling you it was called a "wishing rock." With a smile, you pick up the rock and put it in your pocket. You never know when you might need to make a wish.

You reach the building quickly. To your surprise, the door to the building is unlocked.

"Hello?" you call out as you enter. No one replies. The

building is empty, and yet … it feels not empty somehow. Like you're not truly alone.

"Hello?" you say again, quieter this time. You stand still, holding your breath, trying to hear someone. There's a presence to the building, but when you look around, still there are no other people.

You look around the building. It's really not much more than a small room, maybe ten by fifteen feet. An opening off to the side leads to a circular stairwell, which curves up to the top of the lighthouse tower. A few rustic and timeworn forest green benches line the edges of the room. A small Plexiglas-topped table in the center of the room protects a display map of the land masses in the area that can seen from the lighthouse. Faded old pictures hang on the walls. Along one wall is a door, marked "Storage: Staff Only."

You poke your head up the stairwell. "Hello?" you call out. No one replies.

You walk over to the storage room and jiggle the handle. It turns easily, revealing an empty storage room that is just a few feet deep and maybe six feet wide.

"Not really storing much in this storage room," you mumble.

You step in the room. It's cool inside, but there's a bit of an unidentifiable smoky scent. You look around the walls to make sure there's no smoke coming in from anywhere, but you see nothing. Still, you feel some sort of presence. You trace your hand along the walls, feeling for heat.

"Hello?" you say under your breath.

Suddenly, the entire back wall of the closet separates, two panels pulling apart from the center of a wall that just moments before seemed seamless.

A warm natural light fills the closet.

On the other side of the panels is ... it's incomprehensible. You blink. The building is not this large. This should be the outside of the building. But instead, it's an entire room. No, not a room. A building, and yet it's not a building. There's a sky and there are trees in the distance, but ... but this is not the cliff over the ocean. This is not the island you were on.

A middle-aged man in glasses and a white lab coat rushes toward you. "Well hello, hello, hello! What have we here? Who? Who have we here? Yes, a who not a what, welcome, hello!"

Six teens follow closely on his heels: two girls who look like they're twins, two boys who look like they're twins, another boy, and a girl whose near-white hair and glimmering skin are mesmerizing.

"Hello!" says one of the girls. "I'm Emma. Welcome to the Hub!"

"The Hub?" you say. You realize your jaw has dropped open. Is that a two-dimensional elephant you see far across the field?

"Come on in," Emma says, seeing the confused look on your face. "We'll explain."

You can hardly take everything in as you follow the group toward a cluster of couches and chairs. There are computers and scientists and equipment everywhere within the immediate area of the doorway you entered through. Beyond that there are cabins and a forest, the two-dimensional elephant, and a giant building that seems to be flickering in and out of existence.

"Is that …" you say, pointing to the building.

"Oh that," says one of the boys. "That's the Experimental Building. I'm Charlie." He holds out his hand to you.

"And I'm Chuck," says the one that looks just like Charlie.

"Twins, obviously," you say, laughing. At least that much is clear.

Or is it? The teens exchange glances.

"Actually," says the girl who looks like Emma, "we are twins, but not like you think. I'm Ree, and Chuck and I are twins."

"And Emma and I are twins," says Charlie, clearly delighted that you're all the more confused.

"Wait, what?" you say, looking from one teen to another. You look at the one boy and the one girl who don't look like the others. "Are you … are you twins, too?" Nothing makes any sense.

"No," says the boy, who looks a bit older than Charlie and Chuck. "I'm Ben."

"And I'm Eve," says the other girl, whose skin is so thin it's almost translucent.

"But you're not twins," you say, pointing from Emma to Ree. "And you're not either." You point from Charlie to Chuck.

"Nope. There's a lot to explain," says Emma. "Let's just suffice it to say you've found a place where absolutely everything is possible. This is the Hub, a point where all the universes meet."

"All … all the universes?" you say.

"Yes. And Emma and Charlie are from one universe—the same one you're from, I think—and Ree and I are from a parallel universe. So we're sort of their twins, but sort of not."

"Parallel universes," you say, stunned.

"Yup. With a parallel Earth," says Charlie.

"A parallel …" You don't finish your sentence.

"And Eve is from a different planet altogether," says Ben. "But her planet is in our universe. And I'm just boring me, from Earth."

"Anyway, we were just about to head off on adventure," says Chuck. "Do you want to come with us?"

Continue to the next page to begin this story …

WHERE THE UNIVERSES CONVERGE

"Or," says Eve, "maybe you'd like to stick around here a bit and learn more about the Hub? After all, the Hub is as infinite as all the rest of the universes. And here, absolutely everything is possible."

You raise an eyebrow. Technically, you understand that infinity is infinity, and something that is infinite can be a subset of something else that is infinite. Still, trying to make it make sense makes your brain hurt.

"That's the second time you've said that," you say. "That absolutely everything is possible here. What do you mean?"

The others all exchange glances, like there's an enormous secret they know that they're about to share with you.

"Does that mean you'd like to stay and explore the Hub?" Chuck asks. "You're sure you don't want to visit other planets? Lands of dinosaur-like creatures? Worlds made of emeralds?"

"Stop," says Emma. "There's plenty of time for both. Especially with Ree around."

Ree nods and looks proud, though you have no idea what Emma means by this comment.

"Yeah, I'd like to check out this place first," you say, somewhat uncertainly. Visiting other worlds sounds tempting, but being chased by dinosaurs does not. At least here, you have some idea of what's ahead. Or do you?

"Okay," says Eve with satisfaction. "What do you want to do first? Maybe visit the Experimental Building?" She points at the building you noticed before, the one that seems to be flickering in and out of existence.

"Or," says Charlie with a gleam in his eye as he wiggles his eyebrows, "do you want to learn how to think things into existence? How to create things using just the power of your mind?"

If you decide to explore the Experimental Building, turn to page 9.
If you decide to try to learn to think things into existence, turn to page 27.

"An Experimental Building," you say. "That sounds interesting. What is it?"

Eve smiles and points at the enormous building in the distance that is wavering in and out of view. "When Dr. Waldo first found the Hub, as he was learning how it all works, he had an idea that he wanted to create an invisible building. The way he tells it, his thoughts were unfocused and full of doubts. He wasn't sure what he was doing or whether it was even possible. Wavering thoughts created a wavering building, he says. What was meant to be invisible is only invisible sometimes."

You've been walking toward the building and are close enough now that you can see a large sign over the front doors: EXPERIMENTAL BUILDING. That is, you can see the sign when the building is visible.

"Does the inside disappear, too?" you ask warily. "If we go inside, are we invisible?"

"Good question," says Emma. "Once we're inside, everything is back to normal. From our perspective anyway."

You reach the building and start climbing up the stairs to the entrance, but then you stop. The steps beneath you have disappeared, and you're left looking like you're floating three feet above the ground.

"Whoa," you say, putting out your arms for balance.

"Don't worry," Emma says as she continues to climb the invisible steps. "Trust your feet. The stairs are still there. Even if we can't see them!"

Cautiously, you lift your foot, kicking forward a bit to find the next step. You place your foot where you believe the step should be, then slowly shift your weight to that foot. The step is completely invisible, yet it's supporting you fully. You have a sense of elation, of climbing through air. Then, the building shifts back into visibility again and you're standing on a solid surface once more. You can see the steps beneath you, and you climb to the top of the stairs. Your elation diminishes but you can't wait to see what's ahead.

"Amazing," you say under your breath.

"Follow me," Eve says with a glimmering smile, waving you through the now thoroughly visible door. She then leads you and others down a tiled hallway to the left.

"So, what's inside here?" you ask. "Is this where they do experiments, I suppose?"

"Sort of," says Ree. "But not the kind of experiments you'd think." She grins mischievously.

You pass a few doors before one on the right catches your eye. "The Secret Garden" is written on a sign above the door in romantic, flowery script. "What's in there?" you say as Eve moves past it.

"It's a garden," Ree says. "Where secrets are planted."

"Oh, of course," you say, as if that should have been obvious.

You read the signs over more doors as you walk along the hallway. "The Passage of Time." "Key to My Heart." "Cloud Nine." "Square One." "Out on a Limb." "Blessing in Disguise." "The Funny Farm." "Musical Chairs." "All Downhill From Here." "In a Nutshell."

"They're … they're sayings," you say. "Right? That's the theme?"

"On this floor, yes," says Ree. "Idioms. Dr. Waldo is fascinated by English sayings from Earth. If you recall that two-dimensional elephant outside, that's because Dr. Waldo liked the idea of the 'elephant in the room.'" She paused. "Well, there's more to it than that, obviously. It's a long story."

You recall the elephant. You'd like to see that, too. You want to hear all the stories. There is so much to discover here.

"So," Eve says at the end of the hallway, turning around. "Did you see anything you like?"

"Anything I like?" you ask.

"Any room you'd like to visit," Chuck explains.

You think back on all the rooms you passed, every one of which intrigued you. "Can we visit all of them?" you say.

Chuck and Charlie nod. "Eventually," Charlie says.

"But how do I even choose?" you ask. The options are endless. Literally. You are certain that as you passed the doors, the signs above some of them were in the process of changing.

"You could start by narrowing it down a bit: are you looking for something fun? Or something thought-provoking?" Emma says.

If you want to see something fun, turn to page 12.
If you want to experience something thought-provoking, turn to page 19.

You know it would be good for your brain to seek out something thought-provoking and meaningful, but right now you just want some fun.

"Fun," you say. "Which rooms are fun?"

Everyone looks to Chuck and Charlie.

"Obviously, we are the fun ones," Charlie says to Chuck.

"Good sir, this is true, and the people, they know it," says Chuck.

In unison, they put their hands to their chins, as if stroking their beards, thinking. Then, also in unison, they point to each other and speak at the same time.

"Long Story Short!" says Charlie.

"Time Flies When You're Having Fun!" says Chuck.

They look at you. "The Long Story Short room, or the Time Flies When You're Having Fun room. We'll start with one of those. What will it be?" Chuck asks.

If you choose Long Story Short, turn to page 45.
If you choose Time Flies When You're Having Fun, turn to page 48.

If you're honest, the door that only you can see seems pretty frightening. "How about …" you mentally flip a coin. "Head in the Clouds," you say.

"Good choice," Eve says.

"But don't you want to see where your secret door goes?" Chuck asks. He taps the wall where you saw the door. "Mysteries, my friend! We want to know what lies behind Wall Number One!"

"Wall Number One!" chants Charlie. "Wall Number One!"

"You just want to see if you could jump in before the door closed," says Ree. "But it's not your room."

"I want a door only I can see," Chuck mopes.

"Maybe one day," Ree says, patting Chuck's arm. She turns to you. "Anyway, let's go show you the Head in the Clouds room." She quickly walks back down the hallway and you scramble to follow. You pass several other doors, but you can't help but keep thinking about the one behind you, meant just for you.

Soon enough, however, you arrive at a door with a cloud-shaped sign over it. Written in a romantic script is confirmation that you're in the right place: "Head in the Clouds," it says.

Ree opens the door and you first notice that the room has a lovely peaceful smell.

"That scent," you say.

"It's my favorite, says Eve. "We worked on it a long time. A combination of vanilla, clove, myrrh, ginger root, and caraway seed. Always makes me feel so calm."

You nod. Already you feel your heart rate slowing, your breathing deepen.

The room is neither bright nor dim but rather just comfortably light, with sparkling lights lining the baseboard and the ceiling. Soft instrumental music that sounds like a song of the universe forms an undercurrent of tranquility in the room. A thick rug covers the floor, and scattered around the rug are several smaller rugs. Surrounding each smaller rug are an assortment of the fluffiest of pillows and blankets in calming earth tones.

"Pick a station," Ree says. She chooses a small area rug for herself and starts settling in amongst the pillows. The others all do the same.

Following their lead, you look around until you find an area rug that calls to you. The one you settle on is a kaleidoscope of shades of turquoise, like all the depths of the ocean. You sit and cross your legs, then arrange the pillows around you. Finally you pull a forest green blanket from the pile. As you touch it, you almost gasp: it's soft, almost impossibly soft. You want to make clothes out of this blanket so you can always have it next to your skin. You feel that all your senses are being indulged and nourished right now. The candle, the lights, the music, the blankets, all of it has clearly been optimized to make you feel the most comfortable and peaceful you've been in … well, maybe years.

You sigh deeply.

"Okay," Ree says. "Are you ready?"

"There's more?" you ask. What could possibly improve on this experience?

"Now we bring in the clouds," Ree says. "I'll tell you in advance because once you have your cloud you won't be thinking much. When I tell the room to bring in the clouds, a cloud will form over your head that will clear all your thoughts. It's like a meditation aid."

"A cloud over my head?" you say, raising an eyebrow. You have images of rain pouring onto you and ruining your little nest of sanctuary.

"Not a rain cloud," Emma says, guessing your thoughts. "A peace cloud, really."

"Ten minutes makes you feel completely ready to take on the universe again," Ben says, as he wraps a tan blanket around his shoulders. "And if you do it regularly it improves your ability to focus."

"All right," says Ree. "Everyone ready?"

Everyone calls out in the affirmative.

"Okay. Room! Ten minutes, please!" Ree says.

You hold your breath. Even though Ree explained it, you still aren't sure what's going to happen. Tiny puffs appear over the heads of your new friends, and you imagine the same is happening over yours. The puffs grow and spread into fluffy white clouds, about three feet in diameter and maybe half as high. Then, the clouds all start to descend. You watch as the clouds surround your friends' heads, until your own cloud gets so low that it covers your eyes.

The inside of the cloud is not dark, much to your surprise. Even though the cloud is blocking out light, it has its own warm white-blue glow from within. And, as promised, there is no rain. Just serenity, tranquility, and absolute peace. The scent you smelled earlier is more intense now, but still pleasant and not overpowering. You feel completely content. Was there something you were worrying about earlier? Worry itself now seems like a foreign concept. The music changes and all you hear are nature sounds: ocean waves lapping at the shore. A quick breeze rustling through trees. Far-off birds calling to each other. Your own breath.

And finally, all you hear is your heartbeat, the rush of your blood through your cells. You can almost hear the oxygen inside you. You have never felt so focused in your life. You feel like you could follow a single blood cell on its entire course through your body, if you wanted.

Your breathing has slowed.

Your heart is strong.

You feel alive. Eternal.

You stop thinking.

A breath in.

A breath out.

A breath in.

A breath out.

Breathe

Breathe

Breathe

...

...

...

The air in front of you starts to clear as the cloud dissipates and you feel like you're coming out of a dream.

Like you were lost in infinity and now you're coming back to solid ground.

Once the cloud is completely gone, you stretch your arms wide. "Oh my gosh," you say. "What just happened?"

Eve stands and starts to twist from side to side. She brings a knee up to her chest, then the other, then she quickly runs in place for a few seconds.

"Amazing, right?" says Ben. "How do you feel?"

You stop to assess. How do you feel? "Refreshed," you decide. "Calm. Good. Free." The feeling of peace is still hanging over you nearly as much as if the cloud were still over your head.

"Remember this feeling," says Emma. "Next time you start to feel anxious or worried, bring yourself back here."

"Literally?" you ask, hopefully.

"Literally, or figuratively," says Emma. "You won't always be able to come back here when you need it." She smiles at you. "But yes, you are allowed to come back."

You have so much energy inside you. Being relieved of every worry that was fogging up your head makes you want to tackle every project, every activity you've ever been thinking of.

"Honestly, I feel amazing. I'd love to see more in the Hub, but right now I want to get home and get to work on some projects. But I can come back, right?"

"You definitely can come back," laughs Eve.

"Then I will," you say. You can't even describe this feeling but you don't want it to go to waste. Eve accompanies you back through the Hub and back to Earth. Before she departs you give her a big hug, and then she disappears into the storage room.

The sun outside the lighthouse is bright. The clouds in the sky are dissipating here, too. The day is new, and your life is just beginning.

THE END

"Hmm," you say. You're feeling dazzled and want to go deeper. "Something thought-provoking, I think."

Eve and Emma look at each other, thinking.

"Maybe Head in the Clouds?" Eve says, tapping her lip with her finger.

"Or At the End of Your Rope," Emma says. "That one is good practice."

They look at you to see your reaction. "How does one of those sound?" Eve says.

But while they've been speaking, you've noticed something strange. Behind them, another door has been flickering in and out of existence. It's there, it's gone. It's there, it's gone.

"Where does that go?" you say, pointing.

Everyone turns.

"Where does what go?" Ree says.

The door has gone out of view again. "Hang on," you say, and you wait for it to flicker back into sight. Filled with anticipation, everyone keeps staring at the blank wall.

"There," you say when the door finally reappears.

"There where?" says Charlie.

"There what?" says Chuck.

"You're looking right at it," you say. "The door. A dark green door."

"I don't see it?" Chuck says. He walks over to where the door is and touches it. "Just a wall, my friend."

"But you're literally touching the door," you say, confused. You look up and read the words on a placard over the door. "Life's width is measured in courage; life's depth is measured in compassion." You feel a shiver run up your spine.

Ben looks at you. "You're seeing a door?" he says. He steps to the wall. "Here?"

The door has again flickered out of existence. "Well, it's not there now," you say.

Ben turns to the others. "Do you remember? Dr. Waldo has always told us there's a room that you can only see if you're ready to see it."

"But if there were, we'd have seen it," Chuck says. "Of course we're ready."

"Maybe it's a different room for each person," Emma says. She looks at you. "Maybe this room is only for you."

"Do I … do I have to go in?" you ask. The shiver returns.

"I don't think so," Emma says. "But I suspect that if you go, you have to go alone."

"So what do you want to do?" Eve asks.

Everyone stares at you, awaiting your choice.

If you want to check out the Head in the Clouds room, turn to page 13.

If you choose the End of Your Rope room, turn to page 21.

If you choose the door only you can see, turn to page 104.

"'**End of Your Rope**' sounds good?" you say uncertainly, but given the choices, that's as good as any.

"Okay," says Emma. "Let's go!" Without checking to see whether anyone is following her, she heads back down the hall and stops at a door not far down on the left. Over the doorway is a placard with "End of Your Rope" written out with ropes.

"Clever," you say, pointing at the sign.

Inside, the room is very simple. A thick rope hangs from a high ceiling, its end dangling about six feet above the ground. Beneath it is a step stool.

"You sure you're ready for this?" Chuck says.

"Um … what exactly is 'this'?" you ask. You're starting to have second thoughts about your choice.

Eve takes your hand and leads you to the step stool. "Up," she says, pointing at the steps.

You climb up, watching the others. Is this a joke?

"Grab the rope," she says. She pauses a moment, then adds, "It's sort of sticky, which makes it easy to hang on to. Don't worry."

You grab the rope and you can feel the stickiness Eve mentioned. It feels almost like it would be difficult to let go.

"Okay, I'm going to move the step stool now, are you ready?" Eve says.

"You mean I'm just supposed to dangle here?" you say. You suspect the fun rooms might have been more … well, fun.

"Yup," says Eve. "Ready?"

You wrap the end of the rope around one of your hands and hang on tight.

"Okay, ready." The ground isn't that far below you, after all. If you fall, you'll only fall a foot or two.

Eve moves the stool far to the side. "Doing okay there?" she asks.

"Just fine," you say. "How long do I do this? And, um, what's the point?" Surely there's a point. Right?

You hear a metallic clunk, and you notice Emma is standing next to a podium, her fingers above a button that you suspect she might have just pushed.

"What does that do?" you ask, but even as the words are coming out of your mouth, you get the answer. The floor below you is separating, revealing a giant hole. The new floor is about three feet farther away, and is covered in thick cushions.

"Um … so … is this … what's … am I …?" You're not sure what to ask. You're starting to feel a little queasy.

"You're at the end of your rope," Eve explains. "This room is about mindset. When you get to the end of your rope, do you give up or do you dig deep inside you?" She pauses. "The stickiness should be wearing off about now," she says. "The rope will be harder to hang onto in a few seconds."

You start to feel your hands slipping. Just as she's said, the rope feels slicker now. How are you supposed to hang on?

The floor below you seems to be inching away.

"Wait," you say, desperately clinging to the rope. "Wait."

"So now comes the mindset part," says Eve. "The rope was never sticky at all. You just thought it was because I told you it was. But it was always exactly as it is now. The question is, can you shift your mindset to make it sticky again? Can you believe strongly enough that you will always have enough rope to get you to the floor? Because if you can, then it'll be true."

You slip a bit more. "I can't change this rope with my mind," you say. "That's ridiculous." You're starting to panic a bit. You can feel the sweat forming on your forehead.

"It's all about mindset," Emma explains calmly. Her voice is soft, soothing. It takes you back from the brink just slightly. She continues. "What do you do when you get to the end of your rope? You hang on. And you believe in yourself. Right?"

"Um, right?" you say. You twist the rope around your hand again. It feels slicker than before. The floor below you keeps moving, inch by inch, farther and farther away.

"The texture of the rope has not changed at all since you first grabbed it," Eve says. "Just the way you think about it. So now's your chance to practice your mindset. Tell yourself the rope is easy to hold onto. Tell yourself you can hang on to it all day if you have to. Tell yourself the rope is even getting longer. This is easy. You believe in yourself."

"Sure," you say. "Sure." But you're not so sure. You close your eyes and inhale deeply, then you start imagining, visualizing the rope. It's easy to hang onto, you tell yourself. It's sticky. And not only that but the rope is getting longer. You have nothing to fear. You have everything you need. You can do this. "I believe in me," you whisper under your breath.

At first, nothing seems to change. But you keep repeating all the positive thoughts. You keep telling yourself it's possible. When a doubt slips into your head you push it away—you imagine a broom, sweeping at the negative thoughts. "I can do this," you whisper. "The rope is easy to hold on to, and I am strong. I have everything I need."

Suddenly the rope does seem just a bit easier to hold on to. It feels sticky again. A surge of hope rushes through you. Then you feel something bump against your chest, your leg. You open your eyes: the rope has grown longer. Long enough, even, that you can easily climb down to the floor without falling. You slowly lower yourself into the pile of cushions, and collapse.

"I did it!" you say. "I did it!"

"Mindset," Eve says, smiling. "You did it!"

Emma pushes another button at the podium. You hear another clunking sound, and then the floor rises back up to the main level. You step out of the cushions and onto the main floor with the others.

You are glowing inside. "I can't believe I did that!" you say. "Really, you didn't help? You didn't make the rope longer?"

"Nope," Eve says. "That was all you."

You nod to yourself. "Nice job, me," you say softly. You give yourself a little high five. "Well done."

"Not that there are never obstacles you have to get through," Eve says. "But a big part of your success always has to do with your mindset. One of your Earth people once said, 'Whether you think you can, or think you can't, you're right.'"

"Henry Ford," Emma chimes in. "That was Henry Ford. The carmaker."

"Whether you think you can, or think you can't, you're right," you repeat. You feel empowered. You feel like you can do anything.

You can't wait to get out into the world and prove yourself right.

THE END

When it comes right down to it, it's your table.

"I want to go," you say, your firm tone conveying more confidence than you feel.

The others exchange glances.

"No offense," says Chuck, "but you haven't done anything like this before. You could end up somewhere dangerous. Believe me," he says, nudging Charlie. "We've ended up in plenty of dangerous places."

Charlie raises his eyebrows and nods solemnly. "That time," he says, looking at Chuck knowingly.

"I'm saying," Chuck says, shaking his head. "How could we have known the entire planet was made of quicksand?"

"I've never done it before," you say, ignoring their digression, "but that doesn't mean I can't do it. After all, have any of you ever created a portal on your first try?"

The others squirm a bit.

"You have a good point," says Ben. "Still, it might be safer for someone else to take the wheel, so to speak, the first time."

You stare at the table, frustrated. That table is causing you a lot of stress. You start to wonder. If you can make things appear out of nothing, surely you can make things disappear into nothing, too, right?

If you try to make the table disappear, turn to page 132.
If you continue to argue your case, 98.

Thinking something into existence. That's impossible, right? These people are just playing with you. You're sure of it. You decide to call Charlie's bluff.

"My mind," you say. "I'd like to create something with my mind." Internally, you laugh. Now they'll have to admit they were just joking.

But to your surprise, no one looks put off. In fact, they look excited.

"Excellent choice," says Emma. She waves an arm toward a cluster of chairs and couches. "Let's sit and fill you in."

Everyone follows Emma and sits, their faces beaming with eager anticipation. Before you're even settled into what may be the most comfortable chair you've ever sat in, Chuck speaks up. "So basically, you just think of something, and it appears."

"Chuck," says Ree, rolling her eyes. "It's not that simple."

"If it were that simple, every time you thought of a herd of donkeys, a herd of donkeys would appear," Charlie says, laughing.

For a millisecond, you find yourself bracing for a herd of donkeys. You breathe a sigh of relief when none appears. And you feel vindicated.

"So it's not really possible, then," you say. You glance at the Experimental Building. Looks like you'll be heading over there soon.

"Don't listen to them," says Emma. "It's possible. It does take concentration, though. And thank goodness Chuck and Charlie are easily distracted because otherwise, yes, we would have herds of donkeys all over the Hub."

Ree nodded. "For sure. So. What would you like to think into reality?"

You're still confused. A herd of donkeys? That couldn't happen, could it? "Um … what are my options?" you say. "What have you guys made before?" Internally, you laugh again. Surely this is all a joke.

"Well, this furniture, for one," says Ree, a smile coming to her face. "We made all of this. Everything here, someone made." She spreads her arms broadly, indicating everything you can see.

"Everything" is a lot of stuff. Not just the couches and chairs but the lab equipment, and also the cabins in the distance, and that giant building that keeps flickering in and out of sight. The mountains. The river. The birds. And that elephant in the distance that you swear is two-dimensional. "You made it all?" You frown. "No, you're kidding me. Where? Is there a factory here, or …? Is that building, is that where you made everything?" You point at the vanishing building just as it pops back into view.

"No, we made it with our minds," Chuck says.

"Speaking of making things with our minds," says Charlie, "whose turn was it to bring snacks?"

"There are no turns," says Ree. "Just people being generous. You're more than welcome to contribute."

"Or," says Emma, turning to you, "maybe you'd like to try? Do you want to think some cookies into existence?"

"Or another table?" says Chuck. "We really do need more tables."

Charlie nods in agreement. "Never too many tables."
Eve raises an eyebrow at this.

"But how is it done?" you ask. It seems impossible, and surely they don't expect you to do it without ever having witnessed it. "I'd like to watch before I try."

"Wanna see?" Charlie says. He's leaning forward, eager to show you something he thinks you won't believe.

You think you won't believe it, too. "Sure," you say.

Charlie closes his eyes. Chuck watches him a moment, then looks at you and nods.

Charlie opens his eyes again. "Wait, what should I make?"

You look from Charlie to Chuck. They seem to be serious. You shake your head. "Whatever. I don't know. A chair?"

"A chair?" Charlie says. "So boring. Okay. A chair." He closes his eyes again and his brow furrows in concentration. He waves his hands in front of himself and grins, eyes still closed.

Then, out of nowhere, a chair materializes. It's a simple chair, like one you'd find in an old schoolhouse, but it's a chair. And it wasn't there before. You look up. Did someone from above drop the chair into place when you blinked? But there's no one there. No walls the chair could have been hidden behind.

"What?" you say under your breath. You look at Chuck and Charlie. They are grinning ear to ear, watching your disbelief. Maybe a trap door? You wonder.

You turn to Ree. "What happened?" you repeat. You don't know what else to say.

"It's the Hub," she says, spreading her again arms to encompass the whole space. "Here, everything is possible."

"Here, everything is possible," you repeat. You've heard that so many times already. But you had no idea what it meant.

"You could do it, too," Chuck says. "Go on, give it a try."

"A table? Or cookies?" says Emma.

Ben, who has been quiet until now, says, "To be honest, I'm rather hungry. My vote is for food."

Emma looks at you. "Well, which would you like to try?"

If you decide to make a table, turn to page 31.
If you decide to make cookies, turn to page 41.

You think hard. Table or cookies? Table or cookies?

"Table," you say, finally. But in your head, you have another plan. They gave you the ideas. Table, or cookies. Maybe whatever magic they're doing, they have all planned out in advance. They ask if you want to make a table or cookies. Somewhere, someone else is ready with a table or cookies. When you close your eyes to concentrate, they'll rush in with the goods you "created with your mind."

You're on to them.

So even though you say "table," in your mind you're thinking up a table unlike anything they've ever seen.

"Go on, then," Chuck prods. "Think it into existence. Four legs, a flat top, you can do this."

It's almost like he's telling you exactly what to think. Your skepticism rises. You try to focus on anything other than what he's just told you, but you find it's a bit like when someone tells you not to think of an elephant, and all you can think about then is an elephant.

Is that how that elephant appeared?

You shake your head and close your eyes. You let your mind go blank.

"Good," says Emma, softly. "Focus on the table. What is it made of? What do the legs look like? Are they square or rounded? Is the table painted? Imagine yourself touching it. Is it smooth? Rough?"

Her voice seeps into your thoughts. You start to imagine a table. Four legs, wood, rounded legs. No—No, you think, that's what they've led you to imagine. Think differently. It's made of wood, yes, you like wood. But it's

... what. It's a cube. A cube with two open sides. The other sides are all solid. The table is large, large enough that you could easily sit inside the opening. It is painted ... no, it's not painted. It's not wood after all. The material it's made from is reflective. Like a mirror, but not glass, something that won't break. You reach out a hand, glide your fingertips across the table top. It is smooth to the touch, smoother than anything you've ever felt before. You walk around the table in your mind and you see that from some angles, because of the mirror finish, it almost disappears. You imagine sitting inside the table. The table, like the closet, is a portal. A portal to other worlds.

Your internal narrative mesmerizes you. Your heart rate slows, as does your breathing. The table is as real inside your mind as any memory. You're not creating the table anymore; you're simply remembering something as true and real as you, as your home, as Earth.

"Woah," you hear someone say. Chuck, maybe?

The sound startles you and brings you back to the present moment, here and now. You slowly open your eyes.

The table you have created, exactly as you imagined it, is now sitting on the floor before you.

"What the heck ..." you stammer. Did it really work? In visualizing the table you put yourself into such a trance that you wonder if you're still inside your head. You blink, take in a deep breath, but the table still is there. And there's no way they could have predicted you'd make a table like that.

This power is real.

"Nice!" says Ben. He walks around the cube, eyeing it carefully from all sides. "From some angles it's almost invisible. Really amazing!" He looks at you with admiration.

You reach out a hand, glide your fingertips across the table top, but you already know exactly what it is going to feel like. Smooth. Smoother than anything you've ever felt before.

"How beautiful," says Eve. Her fingers are resting on the table top. "This surface. It's incredible."

"Is it made of mirrors?" Charlie says. He bends over to look at his own face in the side. "Gorgeous," he says, with a wink to himself.

Chuck leans next to Charlie and stares into the reflection of the two of them, side-by-side. "It's like looking in a mirror." He laughs at his own joke and stands. He looks at you. "Because we look alike, you see. That's why."

You nod. "Yeah, I got that." But your attention is not on the smooth mirror outside of the cube. Your attention is on the inside. If everything else about the table is exactly as you imagined, does that mean that the inside … is a portal?

"You've got a funny look on your face," says Eve. "Everything okay?"

"Yeah, it's just …" You don't finish your sentence. The inside of the cube is exactly as you had imagined it. Big enough for you to sit within the walls.

You lean down. You touch the inside of the cube. You

could swear you feel an energy surge coming from the side of the cube straight into your hand, through your whole body.

The feeling is warm, surging, but yet you jump back as if you were shocked.

You blink. You want to try it. You want to see where this cube might take you.

If you decide to get inside the table, turn to page 35.
If you decide it's best not to, turn to page 38.

The cube of air within the reflective sides of the table almost seems to shimmer. Is that because the reflections are catching the light? Or is it because the table does, in fact, do what you meant it to do? Is it a portal?

The temptation to find out is overwhelming. As the others look on in confusion, you get down on your hands and knees and crawl into the table.

"Um," says Chuck. He squats down to look at you. "Everything okay there, buddy?"

"It's all good," you say, your voice squeezed as your body contorts. You're inside the space and you're sure of it now: there's something special about this table. "I just want to check something out."

Eve kneels to look at you. From her face, you have the feeling she already is starting to put the pieces together. Her words confirm it. "When you imagined this table," she starts. Her words are slow, like she's not sure yet what she's going to say. "When you imagined this table, did you imagine something ... are you checking for something? Is there something inside the table?"

The way your face is suddenly warm tells you you're blushing. You look at your reflection and can see your instinct was right.

"What is it?" Eve asks. "Maybe you should tell us?"

She sits on the floor right next to you and looks at you intently.

"It's nothing," you say.

Eve shakes her head. She speaks quietly. "It's something. Tell me. You're in a safe place here. And if there's something we need to know ... I mean the universes are unpredictable. You don't have a lot of experience with all of this. I don't want you getting into something you can't get out of." She locks eyes with you to let you know she means it.

You feel warm. You glance at the others, who are straining to hear the conversation. You lower your voice so only Eve can hear.

"So, when I was imagining this box, I … well, I wanted to create something unique," you say.

"You wanted to make sure we weren't just fooling you," says Eve.

You let out a small laugh. "Yes. I wanted to know if it was real. So I imagined a table exactly like this. And I imagined that this space might … well, that it might be a portal. Like you say that storage room is." You nod in the direction of the door you came through into the Hub.

Eve purses her lips, like she's thinking carefully before commenting. "So, I totally understand that," she says finally. "But like I said it can be dangerous out there if you're inexperienced. And we don't know anything about what you've created here. It could work just like the elevator—the storage room—or it could … it could work very differently."

"Or it might not work at all," says Emma. You realize everyone has leaned in close enough to hear your conversation. The others all nod.

The space you're sitting in is small and a little uncomfortable. You're starting to regret this a bit. In fact, you're embarrassed and sort of wishing you could just get out of the Hub completely.

You realize that maybe you can. But how? You have no idea how—or if—this table-portal might work.

Is it worth a try?

If you decide to try to get the portal to take you somewhere, turn to page 51.
If you decide to climb back out, turn to page 58.

Emma looks at you. "What's on your mind? Your thoughts are practically screaming."

You blink. "Can you guys hear my thoughts?" you say.

Chuck snorts and rolls his eyes. "Yeah, probably we could but Emma and Ree told us we're not allowed to do that."

"Probably you could?" you say warily. You try to clear your brain of all thoughts. You don't know that you want anyone else seeing what's inside your head.

"Everything is possible here," Emma says.

"Yeah, you've said that," you say. "A lot."

"So, hypothetically, we could read minds here. And we've been to planets where people could read minds," she continues.

"Or worse," Charlie says, shaking his head.

You wonder what "or worse" means but decide not to ask.

"But we agreed it's an imposition of each other's privacy," Ree adds. "So collectively we decided not to try to figure out how to do it." She looks sternly at Chuck and Charlie.

Chuck and Charlie look up to the sky. Charlie whistles under his breath.

"Anyway," Emma says. "What's on your mind?"

You shrug a shoulder. "Well, I didn't just imagine a table," you say.

Eve squints. She leans over to see if there's something behind the table, but sees nothing. "Yes?" she says. "What else did you imagine?"

You feel a bit silly and you squirm. "I imagined that it

would also be a portal. You know, like …" you nod your head toward the doorway you entered through. "Like that."

Chuck and Charlie's eyes light up. "Did you create a portal?" Charlie asks. He gets on hands and knees and pokes his head inside the table. "In here?" he says. He touches an inside wall of the cube, then pulls his hand back immediately. "Whoa," he says. He looks at Ben. "Check this out."

Ben glances at you, then leans over to look inside the cube. He cautiously reaches inside and places his palm on one of the inner walls. He gasps. He squats down, then sits on the floor next to the table, reaches into his pocket, and pulls out something that looks a bit like a magnifying glass without the glass. The part that in a magnifying glass would be a circle is instead a hexagon, and the sides are about as thick as your little finger. The handle is flat and wide, with a small screen. As Ben brings the instrument closer to the table, lights begin to dance on the small screen from the bottom up, starting with just a few cool blue lights and eventually filling the entire screen with green.

Eve bends over to look more closely. "What is that?" she says, pointing at the device in Ben's hand.

Ben smiles, looking a bit embarrassed. "Ah, just a thing I made. Remember when we all were out trying to find other elevators—portals? I thought it would be helpful if we had a tool." He held up the instrument. "So I made one. Portal detector. It's in beta, you might say." He moves the portal detector closer to the table. "But I'd also say it seems to work." He leans back on his heels and looks at you. "I think you made a portal," he says, half question, half statement.

"I made a portal," you say under your breath. It worked!

"Well, what are you waiting for?" Chuck says, sweeping a hand from you to the table. "Are you going to try it out?"

Before you can answer, Ben holds up a hand. "Wait," he says. "It looks like you did create a portal, but that's all we know. It could be unstable. It could be perfect. We should do some tests before any sentient being gets in this thing."

"Spoilsport," says Charlie under his breath.

"Charlie!" Emma says. "Ben is just trying to keep us safe. We're lucky to have some clear heads around here."

But you're caught up in the realization that you actually did make a portal. And you're certain it will work. After all, the table came out exactly as you imagined it; why wouldn't the portal be the same?

"I'd like to give it a try," you say. Everyone looks at you.

Ben shakes his head. "I can't stop you, but I'd strongly advise against it. Just let me do some testing first."

You're sure, though. You're sure you're right.

If you decide to try out the portal, turn to page 43.
If you agree to let Ben do some testing, turn to page 62.

Now that you think of it, your stomach is grumbling, too. You wonder, briefly, how long you've been there. Does time in the Hub move at the same speed as time on Earth? What, really, is time?

Your brain definitely cannot process all of this without some food.

"Cookies," you say. "I'd like to create some cookies."

"Excellent choice," Chuck says. "What kind?"

"Umm… chocolate chip?" you say.

"Chocolate chip are so overrated," Charlie says. "What about snickerdoodle?"

You think for a moment. "If I have to create cookies by imagining them, I think I can imagine chocolate chip cookies more easily." If you're honest, snickerdoodles are almost as much of a mystery as time. What is a snickerdoodle anyway?

"Okay, then," says Emma. "Whatever you're comfortable with. So now, close your eyes and imagine everything about chocolate chip cookies. Hold your hands out as if you're holding a plate of them. Imagine how they smell, how they taste, all of it. Imagine it like they are as real as you are."

You close your eyes and start visualizing as best you can. The smell, how you pick it up at the back of your nose and how it could make you come running from a block away. The taste, the sweetness of the chocolate and a slight saltiness to the cookie. The texture, the creaminess of the chocolate contrasted with the chewiness of the base. You imagine the weight of the cookie-laden plate in your hands. You hear the sound of yourself humming with delight. The image is vivid in your mind. Your mouth is watering.

If you think it's going well, turn to page 71.
If you're not so sure, turn to page 74.

"I'm going to do it," you say, stepping forward. You feel an unfamiliar sense of courage. Some might call it bravado but you trust your gut on this.

Ben shakes his head. "I really can't recommend that," he says. "So much could go wrong."

"I know it's going to work," you say. You don't want to let doubts slip in. Believe and make it happen, you think.

"You could well be right, but there's value in testing," Ben says.

You won't be deterred. You shake your head and wave a hand for Ben to step aside. He does. You climb into the table. Your knees are up to your chin. You wish you'd imagined a slightly larger table.

"If you insist on going, please put this on," says Eve, pulling a bracelet out of her pocket. "It'll let you breathe wherever you land. If you land somewhere without an atmosphere close enough to Earth's."

You aren't sure you understand, but you put the bracelet on. You nod your thanks.

"How does it work?" Emma says. You suspect the uncertainty in her tone is about whether she thinks it will work at all, much less how.

You don't answer. Instead, you let your instincts guide you. You place both your palms flat against the surface in front of you, and you close your eyes. You feel a tingle in your hands that surges up through your arms.

Where to go? Your mind whips through ideas: Somewhere with a breathable atmosphere, you think, as you notice the weight of the bracelet on your wrist. Somewhere with mountains. A planet of dinosaurs. Waterfalls. A universe made up of diamonds. Lots of intelligent life. No intelligent life.

I really want to see everything, you think.

You take a deep breath and try to focus.

Turn to page 56.

Mentally you flip a coin. "Long Story Short?" you say. "I guess?"

"Long Story Short it is!" Charlie says. "Good choice, good choice."

Charlie leads the way down the hall. As you pass the rooms again, you wish you could visit them all.

"If you come back," Ree says, "you can visit more of the rooms."

Did she just read your mind? You dismiss the thought, but then you remember that here, everything is possible. Or so they've told you. Would mind reading be possible, too?

One of the doors sits slightly open, and from within the room you hear a bark. You look up at the placard over the door: "Every Dog Has its Day."

"What's in there?" you ask.

Emma stops, and the others stop, as well, to wait. She pushes the door open wider and you marvel at the room, which seems like it's outside. There are no walls, no ceiling; just a wide grassy park and clear blue skies.

Emma points out a couple of people in the distance, wearing white lab coats like Dr. Waldo's. "A few of the research assistants from Lero, the planet Eve is from, fell in love with Earth dogs. They have their own kinds of pets on Lero, but not dogs. Anyway, they are sort of obsessed with dogs. So they made this room. And every day, they snatch a dog from Earth—"

"That makes it sound like kidnapping," Ree says. "Or dognapping. It's not, really."

"Well," Emma continues, "they find a dog from Earth,

one that's living in a shelter, and they bring it here for a few hours. While it's here, the dog is treated to every possible dog delight. Their favorite foods, games, all the fetch they can handle, a ride in a car with their head hanging out the window, tugging on a rope, all sorts of things, and then at the end a magic scrub and trim to get them all cleaned up before they go home, but without any of the fuss or mess."

"Doesn't anyone notice they're gone?" you ask. Today's dog is a sweet chocolate lab. It sees you and you swear you could almost understand what it says as it barks. Its tail is wagging so fast it seems it could motor an engine.

"The assistants return them to Earth at the exact same moment in time that they retrieved them," Emma shrugs.

"But if they're suddenly clean and trimmed…?" you say, your sentence trailing off into a question.

"No one has complained yet!" Eve laughs.

A research assistant inside the room sees you and waves. You wave back. You watch as the chocolate lab chases a ball that seems to be magically throwing itself. After a few throws the lab returns to the research assistant for some petting and hugs, and then it goes right back to the never-ending game of fetch.

Emma waves at the research assistants, then pulls the door shut behind her. "Another excellent room to visit if you're ever stressed," she says.

"Can … we … please … go … now?" Charlie says, mouthing other words between each word, but you can't make out what he said.

Ree rolls her eyes. "Yes, we can go now," she says. "Lead on, Charlie!"

"Follow … me!" Charlie says, as he runs down the hallway.

Turn to page 77.

"Time Flies When You're Having Fun," you say. You don't have a clue what you're getting into, but with "fun" in its title, that room seems like a good option.

"This way," Chuck says, leading you back down the hallway.

You follow, but more slowly: every room you pass continues to intrigue you. Flickering shadows under one door on the left lead you to read the sign above it: "Cat's Out of the Bag."

"What's in there?" you ask, pointing.

Eve smiles. "Oh, I love that room! It's just full of kittens! I go in there a lot."

The next room on the right is labeled "Raining Cats and Dogs."

"It's not really …?" you say hesitantly. It couldn't possibly be a room where it's actually raining cats and dogs. Could it?

"It is," Chuck says.

"But don't worry, they don't get hurt," Emma says, frowning. "I made sure of that. They love it, really, or at least they seem to."

"And they're not real live cats and dogs," says Charlie. "They're imaginary."

Emma sniffs. "Who's to say what's real and alive?"

She makes a good point, you think. "But what's the purpose of these rooms?" you ask as you pass by a room labeled Cloud Nine.

Ree follows your gaze and opens the door to Cloud Nine. Inside is a completely empty room. "For one, play," she says. "Dr. Waldo believes, and I agree, that it's important to remember we all need to play sometimes. And for two, practice. In here, we practice making clouds. Clouds aren't solid and they're not liquid, so they're more difficult. Quite tricky, really."

"First cloud I ever made weighed about fifty pounds," Chuck says, shaking his head. "Good thing it didn't land on anyone."

Ree goes into the room, and the rest of you gather around the doorway. She closes her eyes and wiggles her fingers loosely at her sides. She holds out her hands in front of her, palms together, then slowly pulls them apart. As she does, a small cloud forms between her hands. As she pulls her hands further apart, the cloud grows and grows. Finally she pushes her hands up to the sky and the cloud lifts, still growing. The cloud keeps rising, and you suddenly realize that the room doesn't seem to have a ceiling at all.

"Wait," you say, pointing up.

"Yup," says Chuck. "The Hub. Everything is possible." He shrugs. "Come on, Ree. Time Flies!"

Ree wipes her hands together and looks up at her cloud with satisfaction. "Nice and fluffy, just like I like them," she says. She stares at the sky for a moment, and you swear it turns just a tiny bit more blue.

"Can we go now?" Chuck says.

Ree gives you a sideways glance. "Chuck *loves* the Time Flies room."

"Don't give me that," Chuck says. "You know you love it, too."

Ree nods, the corner of her mouth turning up.

"Maybe I do," she says.

You are even more intrigued. You keep walking down the hall until finally Chuck runs ahead and stops at a door that is covered in hundreds if not thousands of old clock faces, ranging from half an inch to more than three or four feet in diameter.

"Time Flies When You're Having Fun!" Chuck opens the door and you step inside.

Turn to page 100.

Chuck leans over to get a closer look and suddenly you feel overwhelmed. You really do just want to escape. When you imagined the table, though, you didn't imagine any control panels for it. You decide your only bet is to mind-meld with the table. You close your eyes and put your hands flat against the surface in front of your knees.

"Wait," says Eve, sensing what you're trying to do, but you ignore her.

You imagine a planet in a universe far, far away. Somewhere with a wide, warm sandy beach, the waves gently lapping at the shore. In your mind you can feel a soft breeze on the air. It brings with it the salty scent of the sea, and a whiff of mangos, coconut, tropical flowers. The waves tap at the sand with the same rhythm as your heartbeat. You can practically hear the leaves of the palm trees rustling in the wind, the call of the seagulls overhead. You flinch as you imagine a tiny crab scuttling over your toe. You turn your head slightly, toward where the sun is in your vision, and you feel its warmth on your face. This place, wherever it is, is completely real.

"Let's go," you whisper inside your mind. "Take me there."

Did it work? Turn to page 52.
Or, to see if it worked, turn to page 60.
Or, maybe, turn to page 73.
Or, perhaps, turn to page 82.
Or maybe even turn to page 87.

Your eyes are still closed, but your other senses tell you the table has taken you somewhere else. A warm breeze lifts your hair. The scent of the ocean fills your nose. You hear some kind of bird in the distance, and another, returning its call. You lick your lips, and taste the salt of the sea.

You inhale. You feel both calm and elated. Everything is possible, you think. As you open your eyes you see a scene before you that is exactly as you imagined it to be. From the clear blue skies to the wide stretch of sand, this beach is all that you hoped for, and more.

You wish you'd thought to bring a blanket with you, but that doesn't stop you from lying down and stretching out directly on the sand. You're tired, as tired as if you hadn't slept for days. Keeping your eyes open is nearly impossible. The wind tickles your face as you fall into vivid dreams, somewhere between sleep and reality.

"Hey!" you hear. "Hey!"

You blink rapidly. Are you still asleep?

It's Chuck. Chuck is now on the beach, standing before you, an incredulous look in his eyes.

"Hey, wake up!" he says.

You rub your eyes and realize all of them are now standing there, watching you. You sit up, embarrassed.

"How did you all get here?" you ask. You brush sand from your cheek, run your fingers through your hair.

"How did we get here?" says Charlie. "What do you mean?"

"This planet," you say. "How did you get here?"

The teens exchange puzzled glances. "We didn't get

anywhere. You — Where do you think you are?" Ben says.

"On another planet?" you say, but it's a question. Now you're not so sure.

Emma kneels down next to you and puts a hand to your forehead. "Seems normal," she says to the others.

You brush her hand away. "What are you talking about?" you say. "We are clearly not in the Hub anymore."

"That's just the thing," Eve says. "We are in the Hub. But …" she looks around. "But you changed it."

Now she has your attention. "What do you mean I changed it?" You stand up and brush more sand off your clothes.

"You were sitting inside the table," Charlie says, "when suddenly this all started appearing. The sand, the ocean, the sky, the palm trees … all of it. And everything that was in the Hub got pushed aside."

"Like a wave," Chuck adds. "Everything was pushed away, like you were single-handedly expanding the inside of the Hub."

"Pushed away?" you say.

"Yeah," Chuck says. He points across the ocean. "Over there, that's where Dr. Waldo and the lab are. But you pushed it all so far away you can barely see it from here anymore."

You squint and try to see what he's pointing at. You decide that maybe, just maybe, if you use your imagination, you might be able to see people in the distance. On the other side of the water.

As you watch, a speck on the horizon seems to be getting larger and larger. Suddenly you realize it's one of the people on the other side, rushing closer and closer.

Finally, you're able to make out the figure. It's Dr. Waldo, and he's riding across the ocean in a jet ski. He's holding on to the machine with one hand, and with the other he's waving. Even from here, you can tell that he's laughing.

When Dr. Waldo gets close enough to the land, Chuck and Charlie rush into the water to help him to shore.

"This is amazing," you hear Dr. Waldo calling out to you. "Amazing! Simply amazing!"

You are so confused. "I'm not on another planet?" you say. It still doesn't make sense.

"Incredible," Dr. Waldo says, coming forward to shake your hand. He shakes it vigorously, rattling your entire body. "And they tell me you've never done this before? You are not a planet architect?"

"A planet … wait, what?" you say. You wonder if you're asleep.

Emma places a hand on your shoulder. "I know, it's all a lot," she says.

You nod. "I have no idea what's going on."

"What's going on is that you seem to have an extraordinary ability to manifest," Eve says. "You created an entire world in such detail that you even convinced yourself. You have powers we've never seen. And Dr. Waldo, of course, would like to study you."

"Study me?" you say.

"If you're willing," Dr. Waldo says. "Of course, only if you're willing." But from the look on his face you can tell he is extremely excited about the idea.

If you agree to let Dr. Waldo study you, turn to page 66.
If you'd rather not, turn to page 68.

You can feel the energy around you changing. For a moment your courage wavers, but then your whole body starts to feel electrified. You couldn't move your hands from the panel in front of you if you tried. You surrender to the feeling of your body drifting apart into millions of molecules. Then, just as quickly, your body begins to re-assemble itself. The energy you felt in the table winds down and the humming in your ears quiets.

You open your eyes.

You are not in the Hub anymore, but you can't see a thing. Wherever you are, it is pitch dark. There are no stars, no moon or sun, nothing. You start to wonder if your eyes are even open so you physically lift your eyelids. But still, you see nothing.

"Well," you say. "Better luck next time."

You close your eyes again and put your hands out, feeling ahead of you until they touch the inner wall of the table. You wonder for a moment whether you should have listened to Ben. Maybe it would have been a good thing to test out this portal after all. It's too late for that, now, though.

You imagine somewhere very bright. Your mind pops to a lakeside cabin your family used to go to and you smile. Yes, you think. Something like that. You try to en-vision it with every cell of your being, to imagine it into existence.

The feeling begins again, of your body separating from itself and mingling with all of the universe, then the cells coming back together once more and becoming one person again, one individual.

Your heart beats. You're sure it worked this time.

But when you open your eyes, everything around you is still midnight black, not a speck of light.

Your heart is beating faster now. You try one more time. This time you imagine the Hub. You wish you'd listened to Ben. Why did you not listen to Ben? You decided you knew so much more than he did, and look where that got you. Next time, you'll listen to the experts.

You think of the Hub as hard as you can. You imagine your new friends, Dr. Waldo, the lighthouse. Anywhere but here.

Again you feel yourself disassembling then reassembling. Again you open your eyes.

Turn to page 125.

Sheepishly, you shake your head. "It was a joke," you say. You can feel your face burning and your heart beating. "The table doesn't do anything. Just … it was just a joke," you say.

But they're not convinced.

"I don't get it," says Charlie. "What happened?"

"Our new friend, here, made a portal." Chuck looks at you. "Am I right? Did you think a portal into existence?"

You didn't think it was possible to feel any warmer, but you do.

"A portal?" says Ree. "But how? Surely it can't be that easy."

"If it's even possible," says Emma. "No offense," she says to you, "but I strongly suspect you did not actually create a portal."

You frown. How would she know? Who is she, anyway? You're the one who created the table out of nothing. You're the one who was inside it and felt that energy.

Eve looks at you and seems to be reading your mind. "Well," she says congenially, "we are in the Hub, Emma. Everything is possible here."

Emma raises the corner of one lip. "I get that. But to create a portal … it just seems the universes might not want just anyone to be able to create a portal."

"What makes you think I'm just anyone?" you say. The words are out of your mouth before you even think them. You take a breath. "And just how were all the other portals created, anyway?"

Emma blinks, thinking. "Okay," she says finally. "You got me. I don't know."

Ben steps up, diffusing the tension. "So what we may or may not have here is a portal," he says, gesturing toward the table. "I feel like we should find out for sure. For science."

Chuck and Charlie suddenly both punch their right hands into the air. "For science!" they yell.

"Woo?" you say, half-heartedly punching your own hand in the air.

"It's exciting!" says Eve. "But I'm still a little worried about sending someone out into the universes in an untested box, who's never been out there before."

"Could two people go?" Ree says, peering into the space inside the cube. "Eve, you're small. Maybe you and someone else?" She steps a foot into the box, then pulls it back abruptly. "Oh," she says. "There's definitely an energy in there." She looks at you like she hasn't really seen you before. You can almost feel her wondering: just who is this person?

You're feeling emboldened again. You want to step back into the cube and try it for yourself. After all, you made it.

"Maybe Emma should go," says Chuck. "After all, she can get herself home from anywhere."

You bite your lip. You can see both sides.

If you say you want to try it, turn to page 26.
If you decide to support Emma going, turn to page 80.

The warmth of the sun intensifies, and the sounds of the Hub fade away quickly. Slowly you peel open your left eye, then your right.

It worked! You're on a sunny beach, exactly as you imagined. The sky is blue, a brighter blue than you've ever seen, without a whisper of a cloud. The sun on your skin is perfect, not too hot, not too cold. The sand is pristine, nearly white. The turquoise sea is calling to you, inviting you to take a dip in this most private of beaches. This entire beach, perhaps the entire planet, is yours and yours alone.

You uncurl your body and crawl out of the table. You take off your shoes and let the sand caress your feet and between your toes. For a moment you wish you'd thought to bring a blanket. But before you have much time to dwell on the idea, you hear a sound that perks up your ears.

You turn. The sound seems to be coming from a stand of palm trees. You hold your breath so as to hear better, but the sound doesn't repeat. But then you hear it again.

This time, there's no doubt what caused the sound. In the seconds before the creature reaches you, the word "Megalosauripus" pops into your mind, the name of a terrifying, carnivorous dinosaur you once learned about in science class. Is this a Megalosauripus, or merely something like it? Is this your own planet, Earth? Did you travel back in time? Or does another planet somewhere in another universe have creatures similar to the dinosaurs that once roamed your own planet? Where did you land—or when?

As you feel the hot breath of the creature on your face, you realize you will never know.

THE END

You see the look on Emma's face. She has a look that says, "You're an idiot if you try that out without testing it first."

"I guess maybe we should test it first," you say, with a nod at Ben. "But really, what are we testing for? What could go wrong?"

"You said it yourself," Emma says. "That we say it all the time: everything is possible. That means that everything bad is possible too. What could go wrong? What couldn't go wrong?"

"It could make your head explode," says Charlie.

"It could cause a rash," says Chuck.

"It could make you split into two people," says Charlie.

"Technically not the worst thing that could happen," Chuck says, nudging Charlie, pointing out that the two of them are the same person.

"Sometimes, the best thing that could happen," Charlie confirms with a serious nod.

"It could send you off into another universe with no way back," says Ree, a bit more serious.

"It could blow you to smithereens right here in the Hub," says Chuck, whose imagination is really starting to warm to this exercise.

You hold up a hand. "I get it. I get it. Let's test."

Ben nods approval. "Yes. Let's. Now the question is, how exactly do we test to see if something is a portal, without putting a live creature in there?"

Chuck looks around and sees a bowl of fruit on a nearby table. He picks up an apple and puts it in the center of the space inside the table you have created, looking very pleased with himself.

"Okay," says Ben. "But an apple can't operate the controls of the portal."

Charlie sticks his head into the table. "Where, exactly, are these controls that you think the apple is supposed to be operating?" He mumbles. He runs his hand over all sides of the table's interior, then looks at you with a question in his eyes.

You bite your lip. "I guess I thought I'd ... control it with my mind?" You shrug. You're new at this. How were you supposed to know?

Charlie pulls himself out of the table again, and Ben crouches down next to him. He pokes at the apple absentmindedly, then looks at you. "Well, maybe you could still do that, just from outside the table?"

You frown. Why not? It could work. Couldn't it? "Okay," you say with more confidence than you're feeling.

"Everyone get clear of the table," Ben says, though the others are already backing away, which makes you a bit nervous. What, exactly, are they expecting?

Once everyone is well clear of the table, Ben looks at you, waiting. "Whenever you're ready," he says.

You inhale. Whenever you're ready ... what? How exactly *did* you imagine this portal would work? Well, you tell yourself, if you created it with the power of your mind, then it must operate that way as well. You stare at the apple inside the table, then let your focus loosen so you're both looking at the table and not looking at the table, seeing the apple and not seeing the apple. You do the same with your ears, letting all the sounds around you fall into a blur, a background murmur. You become extremely aware of your breath, and of how your breath creates an exchange of molecules from within you to outside of you, from outside of you into the lungs of the people around you. A breath that, ultimately, is shared by the universe, by the atoms swirling inside and around the table, by the cells of the apple.

Then, you start to imagine another planet. You're not sure where it is, but if everything is possible in the Hub, doesn't that mean that whatever planet you're thinking up in your head could actually exist? You imagine this table and the apple within it disappearing, its atoms and molecules separating then reconnecting together to form this same table and the same apple, worlds away on this other planet. You close your eyes and visualize the table becoming invisible here, before you, then reappearing on another planet. You imagine the planet: it is lush, green. The skies are blue. There are no people there. Just this table and this apple …

You sniff. Is something burning?

Slowly all the noises that have been blurring together around you start to differentiate and your brain starts making out words again. You open your eyes and see Charlie and Chuck have grabbed pillows off a nearby couch and are taking turns whacking at a small fire inside the table.

Once the fire is out, Chuck turns to you. "Buddy, if

your plan was to make apple pie, I think we're on to something here."

Your eyes are wide. That pile of burned matter inside the table could have been you.

"Well, then," you say, after a moment. "All's well that ends well. Good thing we tested. So. What else is there to do around here?"

Ree smiles, hooking her arm through yours. "We'll show you," she says. "Where do you want to begin?"

THE END

What the heck, you think, you're curious too. If they think you have an extraordinary talent, well, you'd like to know more!

"I'd love to work with you, Dr. Waldo," you say. "Where do we start?"

Dr. Waldo looks around, laughing. "A good place to start, my friend, might be for you to see if you can reverse what you've done? Not that what you've created here isn't lovely. Perhaps we can find a better place for it."

"A better place?" says Chuck. "A place outside the Hub?"

"Well, yes, that's one place," Dr. Waldo says. He turns to you. "One thing we might study is whether you can actually create a world out there in the universes, rather than only here, where everything is possible."

"Like, create a whole actual real live planet? You think I could do that?" You are stunned. He must be joking. You must have misheard.

"Who knows?" Dr. Waldo says. "Everything is possible! Everything is possible, my child!"

You shake your head. You look around at the beach scene before you. You still can't quite believe that this exists within the Hub. That you created all of this just by imagining it. Dr. Waldo asked whether you can reverse it. Can you un-imagine what you've created? You decide to give it a try.

You close your eyes and breathe slowly, like you once learned when someone was teaching you how to meditate. You breathe in for four counts, hold your breath for four counts, breathe out for eight counts, and then repeat that until you feel centered. If the others are talking, you don't hear them. All you hear is the sound of the waves on the shore, the beat of your heart, your own breathing.

You're not sure how to go about reversing what you created, but you decide to visualize the whole beach shrinking into one spot at your feet, and to imagine the Hub as it existed before—the lab area with its long tables and various electronics, the lounge and all the comfortable couches, the cabins in the distance. In your mind you imagine a vacuum that is sucking up the beach like a vacuum cleaner hose might suck up a blanket, everything rushing in from the sides and toward the center, pulling the original Hub closer to you from the edges. The sand, the beach, the ocean, the trees, you picture all of it being pulled into a vacuum cleaner, restoring the Hub to the way it was when you first arrived. Finally the last bit of beach disappears into the vacuum cleaner in your mind and the Hub is as it was before.

You open your eyes.

"You did it!" Emma says joyfully. "That was amazing!"

You look around. Everything is exactly as it was before. Except now, at your feet sits a small hand-held vacuum cleaner. You stare at it for a moment.

"Is it … is the world in there, now?" you ask.

"Your powers of visualization are far beyond any I've ever witnessed," Dr. Waldo says excitedly. "We have so much to discover! This is incredible!"

You smile. You can't wait. "Well, then," you say, "let's get started."

THE END

You have the strange feeling that you're suddenly a subject under a microscope. You don't mind being the center of attention sometimes, but this feels like a bit too much.

"Nah," you say. "No thanks."

The waves lapping at the shore of the beach you apparently made with your own mind are the only sound, although the awkwardness of the moment is tangible.

"Well, then," Dr. Waldo says, his disappointment clear. "Well, then. I suppose I'd best get back to work." He looks at the jet ski but shakes his head. "No time, no time," he mutters, and then he closes his eyes for a moment, seeming to concentrate. Next thing you know, he is flying, fast as a rocket, back toward his lab.

"Did he just …?" you say.

"Yeah," says Chuck. He, too, seems disappointed. "The Hub. Everything is possible here." He shrugs. "Anyway, we should get you back to Earth."

You look around. You weren't ready to go, but apparently you're being shown the door. "But—" you start, but you don't know what to say.

Emma is gazing across the wide ocean you created. "The elevator is way over there," she says. "Why don't I just give you a ride home from here." It's a statement, not a question. She reaches her hand out to you. "Hold my hand," she says.

Hesitantly, you reach out and hold her hand.

"Hang on," she says. "This will be quick."

What will be quick? You have no idea, but you hang on tight.

Emma closes her eyes and concentrates. After a moment you start to feel a little dizzy, a little nauseated. You close your eyes. It feels like everything around and inside you is spinning. You grasp Emma's hand tighter though you no longer can really feel it; you merely have a sense that her hand is still there. It feels like your whole body has turned to liquid, or even gas; you no longer have solid form. You try to inhale but you don't have lungs. You are in the ocean. You are in the sky. You are everywhere …

And then suddenly, involuntarily, you are gasping, filling your lungs with air. You can feel you have a form again. You are solid. You feel Emma's hand in yours. It feels slippery; one of you has been sweating. Probably you, you think.

You open your eyes. You are back inside the lighthouse.

Emma looks you over to make sure you're okay. "All good?" she says.

You gently slap your shoulders, your chest, your legs, to make sure everything is back where it belongs. "All good," you say.

"It was nice meeting you," Emma says, and before you have a chance to reply, she's gone.

You sit down on a bench along the wall. What just happened? Was any of that real?

And you start to get curious.

Did you actually create a world inside the Hub?

And could you do it here?

You close your eyes. Once again you focus on imagining a beach, exactly as before. You visualize the sights, the sounds, the smells, the feel of the sand, the taste of the salty air. You imagine it with every cell of your body.

You open your eyes.

Nothing has changed. You are still just alone inside the lighthouse.

"Oh well," you say, and you stand up, ready to go home.

Then you see it: at your feet, a tiny seashell that you're sure wasn't there before.

You stare at it for a long time.

Did you create that?

You pick it up and look at it. It feels warm. It has an energy to it that is palpable.

You smile. You put the shell in your pocket.

You head back to your cabin, ready to do some experiments yourself.

Maybe the magic isn't in the Hub, you think.

Maybe the magic is inside you.

THE END

Suddenly, you sense that the weight in your hands is no longer imaginary. You open your eyes and almost drop the platter in astonishment. There in your hands, exactly as you visualized them, are chocolate cookies. You can see the chocolate is still melting—the cookies are literally still warm from the oven.

Your hands are shaking, so you put the platter down on the table. Chuck and Charlie instantly dive in.

"Oh wow," Chuck says through a mouthful of cookie. "You're an excellent chef."

"Mmmm," Charlie agrees, nodding.

Emma shakes her head. "I was going to suggest that we should test to make sure the cookies weren't toxic or something before the boys ate them, but ..." She shrugs.

Out of the corner of your eye you see a white flutter moving toward you. You turn and see Dr. Waldo approaching quickly, his eyes on the cookies.

"Well, well, well!" he says, and then he inhales deeply to get the full scent of the cookies. "To what do we owe this delight?"

Eve beams. "Our new friend here is learning how to create things from nothing here in the Hub."

"Oh, yes, wonderful!" Dr. Waldo says. "And how are we doing?" he asks you, but his eyes keep returning to the tray of cookies.

"So far so good?" you say. "I mean I guess you can be the judge?"

Dr. Waldo picks up the plate, causing Chuck and Charlie to protest loudly. "Yes, yes, I can! An experiment, then! Let's try this." He closes his eyes for a moment and then a tall table appears in front of him. On top of the table is a box. Dr. Waldo opens the lid and puts the cookies inside, then shuts the box.

"All right, the cookies are now hidden away, much to the Charlies' dismay," he says, chuckling. "So now, let me ask you, my friend: Did you actually make cookies?"

If you say yes, turn to page 85.
If you say no, turn to page 93.

There's a shift in the space around you—you're sure of it. Did you just hear a seagull? Is there an ocean saltiness to the air?

You open your eyes.

Everyone is staring at you.

Chuck looks at Charlie, then back at you. "You okay there, buddy?" he says.

You clear your throat and try to ignore the fact that you can feel blood rushing to your neck and face, undoubtedly making you look like a tomato. "Yeah, all good," you say.

Eve, however, is still concerned. "Did you fall asleep?" she asks.

You crawl awkwardly out of the table, stretching as you stand. "No, nope," you say. "Just did a little meditating. You know. Everything was feeling overwhelming so I thought, good time to clear the mind." You move your neck side to side like you're trying to loosen it up. You can see Eve's still skeptical but you ignore it. "So," you continue. "Someone mentioned an Experimental Building?"

Far across from the lounge, the Experimental Building is still standing, large and impressive, except for the moments when it completely disappears from view.

Emma loops an arm through yours. "Yes," she says. "Let's go show you the Experimental Building."

Turn to page 9.

Without your realizing it, your mind has started to wander away from the cookies. You're now thinking about dinner, and the fact you need to get home soon. Now you're thinking about a project you're working on that needs attention. Now you're wondering about the lighthouse, how it became a portal. Who put it there? Oh wait, cookies, you think. You imagine the cookies again. You think about how your grandmother loves to make cookies. They are delicious. She makes big batches and freezes them so every time you go to her house there are cookies available. Every kind, not just chocolate chip but also molasses cookies, sugar cookies, what she calls monster cookies … why does she call them monster cookies? You laugh at the memory. Your grandmother is one of your favorite people. Her smile and her eyes always light up when you see her. You have a photo of her in your house that always makes you laugh, in which she's making a funny pose …

Your thinking is interrupted by a bit of a commotion. You open your eyes.

There, before you, is your grandmother. Except it's not your grandmother; it's a two-dimensional replica of your grandmother, making the exact pose from the photograph you were remembering.

"Um," says Emma.

"That's not cookies," Charlie says, disappointed.

"Who is that?" Chuck says.

"That's my grandma," you say with dismay. "My flat grandma."

"Definitely not cookies," Charlie says.

"I got distracted," you say. "I was thinking about my grandma and her cookies. Then I thought of a photo of her ..."

"Did the photo of her happen to look anything like this?" Ben says.

The two-dimensional representation of your grandma waves, and her smile curves upward, a line on a sheet of paper turning into a half moon.

You wave back.

"Hi, Flat Grandma," Chuck says. He focuses for a few moments on a table, and then a pile of fresh chocolate chip cookies appears. He turns to you. "Don't mean to steal your thunder, friend. I just was all ready for cookies and now I need a cookie." He and Charlie attack the plate of cookies like they haven't eaten for weeks.

Meanwhile, Dr. Waldo has made his way over.

"Who have we here?" he says, assessing Flat Grandma with a bit of confusion.

Flat Grandma winks at Dr. Waldo.

"That's ... that's my grandma," you say sheepishly. "I was trying to make cookies."

"Oh yes, of course, of course," says Dr. Waldo. "Easy mistake. The mind follows trails, it does, weaves and wanders, so easily. But no worry, child! This is easily remedied!"

"It is?" you say.

"Indeed! Just a matter of training the mind. We'll get you meditating for a bit and then in no time you'll be making cookies from the air! No time at all!"

Dr. Waldo wraps an arm around you and leads you to

a small building where he introduces you to a meditation instructor. Flat Grandma follows and stands at the side of the room watching while the instructor takes you through your first meditation practice. After that you return every day to learn to meditate, and within weeks you have enough command of your focus that you can create anything you like in the Hub. Once you're sure of your skills you create a small cottage for Flat Grandma, and she lives there for the rest of time, baking flat cookies and freezing the extras for whenever you come to visit.

THE END

As you trot along behind the others, you run a bit to catch up to Ben. "Why is Charlie talking that way?" you ask.

Ben shakes his head and laughs. "You'll see," he says.

Finally you reach a door at the hallway with the sign above it proclaiming "Long Story Short." Charlie opens the door. Much to your surprise, what lies behind the door is not a doorway. Or rather, it is a doorway, a hole in the wall, but the hole in the wall is not as tall as the door. Instead, it's not much higher than your knee. The rest of the space behind the door is simply wall.

"If you needed to," Emma explains, "you could push this button here to make the door full height." She points to a button on the wall that is labeled with an "up" arrow. "But we like to crawl."

Charlie is already on the floor, scrambling his way through the hole in the wall and into the room, followed closely by Chuck, Ree, Ben, Eve, and then Emma. You shrug and crawl through the hole as well.

Luckily, the room's dimensions are normal for a room, and you can stand at full height once you're inside.

"Okay, now what?" you say. But only the word "okay" comes out. The other words are lost to the air.

"Wait, what?" you say. "What's happening?" Only the word "wait" can be heard in the room. The rest of your words are stuck somewhere.

Charlie looks at you. "Long ... story ... short," he says, with a wink. In between his words, you can see him mouthing other words, but none of them makes a sound.

"I don't get it," you say. Only the word "I" reverberates through the room.

"Every … fifth … word," Emma says. You can tell she's saying other words in between but the room is somehow swallowing them.

You start to understand. Following the pattern you're seeing, you speak slowly: "So what I'm understanding is only the words that are every that is to say fifth oh my here's another word do you see it can monkey donkey cookie book be be be be be heard?"

The room only lets through every fifth word you say, so what you and the others hear you say is: "So only every fifth word can be heard?"

Chuck claps his hands. "Well … done … mate!" He slaps you on the back. "Good … job!"

"You … caught … on … quick!" says Charlie.

Long story short, you think. The room is literally cutting your story short.

"But how does it do this?" you ask.

"But … this?" the others hear.

"You … It's … and … loud," Emma says.

"I … Chuck … Charlie … can't!" Ree says, chuckling.

You carry on stunted conversations for a while, pantomiming wildly to try to be understood and laughing at what actually is said and heard, until finally Emma points to the short door.

"Shall … leave?" she says.

Everyone crawls back out of the room awkwardly, and Emma closes the door behind you.

"So what's the purpose of that room?" you ask. "Just for fun?"

"For fun," says Emma, "and also it's a good way to practice communication."

"But mostly for fun," says Charlie.

"And speaking of fun," Ben says, "I've got to get back to work. I have a meeting in two minutes about a new gadget I've been working on! It's been nice meeting you. Come again!" he says, and then he runs down the hallway and out of the building before you even have a chance to say goodbye.

"And we need to be getting home, Charlie," says Emma. "Mom's birthday party!"

Charlie slaps his forehead. "I forgot!"

"And same with us," says Ree to Chuck. "Same birthday. Parallel mom. Different universe," she explains to you.

Chuck slaps his forehead. "I forgot, too!"

You squint. It's a lot to take in.

"But ... again ... soon!" says Eve, and for a moment you wonder if the dynamics of the room you were just in have spread. The twinkle in Eve's eye, however, tells you she's just playing with you.

"I will definitely come again soon!" you say.

As you head home through the lighthouse portal you realize you have started to think with an emphasis on every fifth word. You can't wait to return to see what other mysteries the Hub holds.

THE END

You sigh. They're probably right. This is something that is meant for someone with more experience.

"Emma should go," you say.

Emma looks at you. Her eyes soften and you can tell she understands what a sacrifice it is. "Are you sure?" she says.

"Sure, go on," you say. "I'll take it after you break it in."

Emma stares at you for a moment, then nods. "Okay." She turns to the others. "But just very quickly. To a place we know." She leans over to look inside the box, and then she moves a hand around the smooth interior, probing the surfaces, but she finds nothing. "Did you, uh, imagine any sort of control panel or anything?" she says, straightening up again.

You blink. "Um, no?" you say. A control panel. That would have been helpful.

Emma shrugs. "Well, I'm not sure I'm the right person to test it, then. I'm sure I can make the box move, but I couldn't guarantee it was because the box is a portal, or because I moved it with my mind."

"Those darned superpowers," Charlie says under his breath.

Chuck slides into the space inside the table. "Well then, I'll go." He feels around the walls to see if Emma just missed something, but he finds nothing. "No control panel. Okay then. I'll do it with my mind." Chuck slowly puts his hands in front of him, touching the wall. "Oh great table. Table of the Universe. Take me to …" He looks at Charlie.

"That planet we went to last week," Charlie offers. "The one with all the waterfalls."

Chuck nods, then closes his eyes, his hands outstretched before him again. "Oh great table. Take me to the waterfall planet," he booms.

The air is electric with anticipation. Everyone is holding their breaths, watching and waiting. Chuck opens an eye and sees he's still sitting in the same space. He closes the eye and tries again. "Table of the Universe. Take me to the waterfall planet."

You feel a shimmer of energy. An image flashes in your mind: you see a lush forest, and close by you can hear water rushing. The image shifts and now you are in a field, staring at a waterfall that must be ten stories high. No, not just one waterfall, you realize. There's another waterfall just to the left of the one you've been looking at, and farther to the left, another, and another. They are all spilling down off a ledge far in the distance, down into a river that is rushing away from you toward some distant ocean. You can almost feel the spray of the falls.

"Hey, table?" Chuck says. "Anytime now." His eyes are open now and he is staring at himself in the mirrored wall within the cube.

You blink, realizing you are still in the Hub.

Finally, defeated, Chuck climbs out. "I give up. It's not a portal."

You're not so sure, though.

Maybe it didn't work for Chuck.

But you think it might work for you.

If you speak up, turn to page 157.
If you decide to just climb into the table and try, turn to page 163.

You open your eyes and find before you the most beautiful beach you've ever seen. The pristine white sand stretches as far as the eye can see to your right and left. Gentle ocean waves lap at the shore. Something that looks like a great blue heron is standing in the shallow surf, patiently awaiting an unsuspecting meal. The sun is high in the cloudless sky; its heat warms your skin without being too hot. The fresh air fills your lungs and the oxygen makes your fingers tingle. A soft breeze caresses your cheek. The table you created has landed next to a large, smooth, pink-and-beige boulder, a few yards away from a cluster of coconut trees. You look up and see fuzzy coconuts clinging to the top of the trees.

"It worked," you call out to the heron. "It worked!"

The heron ignores you.

You crawl out of the table and sit on the boulder for a while, thinking of nothing but the sights and sounds around you. Your nose detects a sweet floral scent, and you discover a clump of tiny flowers on the other side of the boulder. After a while you notice an island or other land mass far in the distance across the ocean.

"Paradise," you say out loud. You have discovered paradise.

Your stomach rumbles. You realize you're hungry. You search your pockets, already knowing they're empty. You hadn't exactly planned on this.

"Paradise isn't paradise if you don't share it," you say to yourself, and you crawl back into the table. You squeeze your eyes shut and hope you can get back to the others. With all of your might, you imagine being back in the

Hub, with Dr. Waldo, Emma, Ree, Charlie, Chuck, Eve, Ben, all the scientists, the lounge, the lab tables, that Experimental Building and the cabins in the distance, all of it. You let the images of the Hub swirl around in your head until all your senses are filled with nothing but the Hub.

You open your eyes.

Everyone is staring at you.

"What just happened?" Chuck says. His jaw drops.

You crawl out of the table and stretch. "I, um, I created a portal."

"You created a portal?"

Ben is waving at Dr. Waldo to get his attention. Dr. Waldo comes running over.

"Dr. Waldo," Charlie says as the older man approaches. "Is it possible to create a portal? An elevator?" He waves a hand in your direction. "Our new friend here created this table, and says it's a portal."

"It's a portal," you say. "I just went to a beach somewhere."

They stare at you.

"Everything is possible?" you say. "That's what you told me?"

They stare at you.

"Yes, but creating a portal?" Chuck says. "I did not know that was possible."

You shrug. "Well, you didn't tell me that. I didn't know it was impossible. So I did it."

Dr. Waldo suddenly starts dancing, arms and legs flailing with joy. "Yes!" he says. "Yes, yes, yes, children! Beyond the limits of imagination! We think it, we create it! Sometimes that is what it takes to get something done, you see! Someone who doesn't know that what they want to do is impossible!" He is humming and dancing, and starts tapping his feet and clicking his fingers. "Flamenco dance," he explains, wiggling his eyebrows, clearly proud of himself. "I'm taking classes."

Dr. Waldo straightens up and rearranges his face to look serious. "Ahem," he continues, clearing his throat. "Anyway. You," he says looking at you, "have done something amazing here. I have questions. Would you be willing to stay with me a while and chat?"

You hesitate. If you're honest, you're feeling a little tired. Apparently creating a portal to other worlds takes a bit of energy.

If you go with Dr. Waldo, turn to page 92.
If you decline, turn to page 96.

You're confused. Is this a trick question? You saw them. Chuck and Charlie ate them. Of course you made cookies.

"Um, yes?" you say.

Dr. Waldo opens up the box and pulls out the plate, still brimming with delicious cookies.

"Very good, very good!" he says. "Matters of the mind are not simply a matter of mind and matter. Me must mind our matter and it matters that we mind!"

He looks so triumphant and proud of himself that you don't want to admit you have no clue what he's talking about, so you just nod.

Your nod must not have been very convincing, though, because Dr. Waldo shrugs and tries again. "You see, the mind matters but matter minds the mind. What I mean is that it is not simply about creating something but about fully believing in the reality of what you created. After all, what is real? How do we know? Nothing comes from nothing, so it therefore must come from something, and that something is real, so the nothing that you created is also a something not a nothing. You see?"

You nod again. "Sure," you say. You don't want to be rude.

"Yes, yes, yes," says Dr. Waldo. "A quick learner, you are. Say, it occurs to me that we could use someone like you on our science team. The scientists always need someone to help create things for their experiments. Would you perhaps be interested?"

You don't even have to think about it. "Yes!" you say eagerly. The idea of spending your days here in the Hub, learning about the universes and science, maybe making some discoveries yourself, sounds like a dream come true. "Do you think I could create a whole planet?" The words come out of your mouth without your even thinking them first.

Dr. Waldo laughs. "Maybe, my friend! Maybe! After all, here in the Hub …"

As if on cue, you and all the others join in to finish the scientist's statement:

"Everything is possible!"

THE END

You've been imagining the sun on your face, but now the warmth feels real. You wonder if your imagination is that good, or if you managed to make the jump to another place.

Slowly, you open your eyes.

There before you is the pristine beach of your dreams. The white sand is silky soft. The ocean is clear and turquoise blue. A small, green lizard-like creature—it closely resembles the anoles you once saw on vacation in Hawaii—scurries by, stopping once to look at you before hurrying away.

Climbing out of the table, you're amazed that you don't feel cramped. After all, you traveled thousands or millions or billions of miles! You smile. You wonder if there's a way to know how far you've come. You make a mental note to ask the others when you get back to the Hub.

As you step out, you realize your little table portal has landed on top of a pile of boulders and is perched somewhat precariously. You step carefully and make your way down the rocks using both your hands and feet.

When you reach the sand, you take off your shoes. You close your eyes and wiggle your toes. The sand is so soft it almost feels like liquid.

A sudden breeze brings with it the scent of something sweet. You inhale deeply. A flower, maybe, you think. You go in search of it, heading inland, away from the water. Soon you come upon the source: flowers with large pink-orange petals, opening out to the sun. Insects are buzzing around them, as drawn to the scent as you were. The flowers are growing in a large cluster next to a small stream tumbling over river rocks, heading to the ocean. The sun is beaming down on a grassy area next to the flowers, and the combination of the warmth of the sun, the heady scent of the flowers, and the calming bubbling of the stream start to make you drowsy.

"Just a few minutes," you think, as you lie down for a nap.

Almost immediately you fall asleep. You dream of waves crashing against the shore and of the chatter of exotic alien birds.

When you wake up, another of the lizard-like creatures is sitting next to your head on the grass, staring at you. You startle, and it runs away.

"What time is it?" you say, though you realize instantly that the question is irrelevant as you don't even know what time is on this planet. Regardless, you think your new friends might be missing you. The sun is lower in the sky, but there's also a new, dim glow by the horizon. On looking carefully, you realize the source: a second sun. It is much smaller and not nearly as strong, but it makes you happy nonetheless.

"This place is amazing," you think. You can't wait to tell everyone about it.

You walk back to where you left the table, but at first you can't find it. Then, with horror, you see it: it has fallen off its perch atop the rocks and is lying at the base, broken, in pieces. Shattered.

"No!" you cry out as you run to the table. "No!"

You spend what feels like an hour—though you have

no idea, because what is time here?—trying to put the table back together, but you have no luck. You kick yourself for not telling anyone what you were trying, where you were hoping to go. Can they find you? Will they even look?

The first sun has now dipped below the horizon, and the second is nearly overhead. It is giving off far less heat or light than the other did, and you imagine this is now what passes as night on this planet.

Your stomach rumbles.

You look around and see there are coconut trees not too far away. You head for the trees, crossing your fingers that you can figure out how to get a coconut down from the top. Then you will look for a cave or something to make a shelter with back by the flowers, on the grass. You hope.

You know that you will never see Earth again. It's time to get busy making your home here.

THE END

It worked!

You have no idea where you are, but you unroll yourself out of the table and stretch. A soft wind blows, carrying the scent of the sea. The sand beneath your feet is white, white as the wispy clouds in the blue sky above you. You kick off your shoes and let the sand sift between your toes.

High above you, you hear birds chirping and you wonder if they're anything like the birds back on Earth. Or maybe it's another creature entirely, that just sounds like birds? You smile. There is so much to discover!

You walk slowly away from the table. Your eyes can't even take in all the sights. Three enormous trees are clustered a bit away from you, behind some giant boulders. You imagine maybe that's where the birds you heard are hiding, but you can't see any. The bark of the trees looks like scales; the leaves at the top look like gigantic feathers. The trees sway heavily left and right making you wonder if the breeze is stronger high up in the air.

You turn back to the sea. The water is crystal clear—so clear you can see the ocean floor as the waves pass. You dip your toes in and savor the feeling.

This is paradise.

You spread your arms wide and close your eyes, soaking in the sun. You start to imagine living here. Surely you could build a house here somewhere. Out of stone, or out of those trees with the glorious large feathers. You'd live off tropical fruit and you'd sit at the beach every day enjoying this peace and calm …

You hear a branch snap behind you. You turn just in time to see one of the trees falling.

Except it's not a tree. It's a tremendous creature of some kind, and it is coming at you quickly. The last thing you see is its mouth, opening wide.

THE END

"Sure, why not?" you say. After all, no matter how tired you get, you may never get this chance again.

"Carpe diem!" Dr. Waldo says. "Seize the day! Wonderful! Follow me!"

You follow Dr. Waldo off toward his labs, but then he takes you to areas of the Hub you hadn't see, could never have imagined. The Hub seems to go on forever in every direction, and you realize that actually, it does.

Over the course of the next few weeks, Dr. Waldo asks you infinite questions, conducts experiments with you, learns from you and teaches you. You go back to the cabin and return to the Hub every day, until it's clear you need to create a little home for yourself here in the Hub. You imagine the perfect cottage, next to the perfect mountain stream, coursing down from the perfect mountain. You literally could not have imagined a more perfect space. Eventually, you become Dr. Waldo's assistant, living out your life making unimaginable discoveries and always remembering that sometimes, all it takes to do the impossible is to simply believe you can.

THE END

You're confused. You did, didn't you? You're sure you did. But why would Dr. Waldo question you? Does he know something you don't?

"Well, I mean, I don't know? No?" you say.

"No?" says Dr. Waldo. He puts a hand on the box's lid. "You didn't?"

"Right? That's what you're telling me? It was all an illusion?" you say.

Dr. Waldo opens the box. It is empty. No plate, no cookies, nothing.

"I see," you say. "I just imagined it."

"No, no, child," Dr. Waldo says. "That's just it—you *didn't* imagine it. That is, you didn't believe. You did create cookies, but when you doubted yourself, they disappeared. It is one thing to create something. It is another thing entirely to believe in it. You must believe in the cookies just as you must believe in yourself."

You're a bit stunned.

"So I did make the cookies?" you say. "They were real?"

"They *were* real, but then you didn't continue to believe they were real, so they vanished," he says. "But no worries. This is a practice, just like any other. All you need to do is practice believing. Would you like to try it now?" he says.

"Sure?" you say, though you're not really sure of anything anymore.

"Hold out your hands," he says. You do, and he gives you the empty box. "Now, close your eyes again, and imagine the cookies again, but this time, don't just imagine them. *Believe.*"

You're not really sure what the difference is, but you figure you'll give it a try. You close your eyes and once again visualize the cookies as if they were real: their taste, smell, how they look, their warm gooeyness on your tongue, how happy the Charlies would be to have them again.

"Sink into it," Dr. Waldo says gently. "Let go. Know that the cookies are real."

You shrug your shoulders but then take a deep breath and imagine that you're not imagining the cookies but rather simply holding a plate of cookies that have existed all along. You start to feel a sense of peace and truth wash over you. The cookies, you know for sure, are back in the box. They are real, and they are spectacular.

You open your eyes. "They're in the box now," you say, handing the box back to Dr. Waldo.

"You're sure?" he says?

"One hundred percent," you say, smiling.

Dr. Waldo opens the box. Sure enough, the plate of cookies has returned.

"Hey, hand that here!" Chuck says. Dr. Waldo complies, and the boys dig into the fresh treats once again.

"I guess you believed," Dr. Waldo says. "And now that you know how to believe, you can do anything." He pats you on the back.

You nod. "I get it now," you say. "I really do." You stop and put your hands on your hips and stare at an empty spot on the floor. Soon, a comfortable looking cot appears, complete with a cozy blanket and a fluffy pillow.

"What is that for?" Eve says, laughing.

"All that believing wore me out," you say. "I believe I need a nap now. But when I wake up, can we do some more of this?"

Eve laughs some more. "Absolutely. You might want to make yourself some ear plugs, though!" she says, nodding her head toward Chuck and Charlie who are, indeed, making quite a ruckus.

You lie down. Before you even have a chance to think about the ear plugs, you are asleep. You dream the strangest dreams, of universes and disappearing cookies and places where everything is possible. Deep within your dream, though, you know every bit of it is real.

THE END

"You know, I'm actually pretty tired," you say. "How about I go home and take a nap, then come back?"

Dr. Waldo nods, but you can tell he's disappointed. "Oh, certainly, certainly. Naps are important! Why, there are days when I have three! Off you go, off you go. Come again when you can!"

"Can I take my table with me?" you ask.

Dr. Waldo purses his lips. "Well, well, you see, I don't know if it will work outside the Hub, but yes, you may." He sort of mumbles it.

"It looks heavy," says Charlie.

"I can carry it," you say, though you're not sure.

You attempt to lift it, but Charlie was right. It's far heavier than you thought.

"Apparently the universes are pretty dense," you say, laughing weakly. You start pushing the table but it seems glued to the floor.

"It seems the table wants to stay here," says Dr. Waldo gently.

"Hmm," you say. You're feeling a little embarrassed now, and a lot tired.

"Go on, take your nap," says Emma. "You can always come back."

You nod. "Okay." You head back to the door to the other elevator, the one that leads to the lighthouse.

"I'll come with you," says Eve. She walks silently beside you, each of you lost in your thoughts. Once you're inside the elevator, it seems neither of you really has anything to say.

Eve taps the control panel and you brace yourself. You

feel woozy for a few moments, disoriented, discombobulated. But then quickly it all passes.

"Home," Eve says, and the door back into the lighthouse lobby opens. A rush of fresh air, smelling slightly of the sea, hits you.

"Okay, well," you say. You step out of the room into the lobby. "Nice to meet you."

"Nice to meet you," Eve says. The door behind her closes again.

You go home and take a nap. You are exhausted and don't dream at all. Or was everything that happened in the Hub a dream?

The next day you think about going back to the lighthouse, but you decide none of that actually happened, and you put it off. You keep putting it off until you simply forget about it completely. You never return to the lighthouse or the Hub again.

THE END

Making the table disappear won't help your cause. "You can't really stop me," you say petulantly. You look at the table. You realize that realistically, they probably could stop you, in a number of ways. Still, you're not sure what to say.

The others exchange glances.

"We probably could stop you," Chuck says, confirming your thoughts. He shrugs.

You shuffle your toe against the ground. Is it ground? You wonder. Does ground indicate that you're on a planet?

You really would like to see some other planets.

"I'm going," you say. You move toward the table and the others part, making way for you. You feel a sudden hesitancy. After all, they know the universes far more than you do …

But you made a portal. If you weren't meant to be able to make a portal, you wouldn't have been able to make a portal. The logic seems clear to you.

You climb into the table as the others watch. It is uncomfortable and small and you wish you'd imagined a table that was just a bit larger.

You feel the others' eyes on you as you sit there, your legs starting to cramp. You wonder exactly how this portal might work.

Or is it a portal at all?

You put the palm of your right hand up against the inside wall of the table and imagine your thoughts pulsing through your arm, through your fingers, and out into the table. You visualize the energy, your life force, pouring out of you and into the universe. You send your thoughts along that energy trail: "Take me to a beautiful island on another planet, in another universe. Take me to a beautiful island on another planet, in another universe. Take me to a beautiful island on another planet, in another universe……"

You open your eyes.

Did it work?

Turn to page 90.
Or turn to page 126.

You try to hide your disappointment. The room looks very bland. A few large clocks seem to have fallen on the black-tiled floor, scattered around the room. But other than that, nothing seems to be very special.

"Huh," you say.

Chuck looks at you. "Just you wait," he says.

You look around. Everyone else looks excited. Maybe you'll give them a chance.

"Okay," you say uncertainly.

"Pick a clock," Chuck says, racing toward a particularly large one lying face up near the far wall. When he reaches it, he sits on it with his legs crossed. The others all find large clocks on the floor and sit on them, so you do the same.

"Okay?" you say.

Chuck can see you're confused, and he smiles. "Charlie, tell us a joke."

Charlie looks up for a minute, thinking. Then he speaks: "What do you call a can opener that doesn't work?"

Chuck groans. "Ah, too easy! A can't opener!"

You chuckle.

You think for a moment that you feel the clock shift under you, but then you think you must have been mistaken.

"Ree!" Chuck calls across to his sister. "Give us a joke!"

Ree is ready. "Did you hear about the two thieves who stole a calendar?" she says.

"Tell us about the thieves who stole a calendar!" Charlie yells out.

"They each got six months," Ree grins.

"Grooooooooaan!" Chuck says, but he's smiling.

You giggle a little, too. And this time, you're sure of it: the clock under you moved.

"What's going on?" you say to Emma, who is nearest you."

"Just hang on," Emma say, smiling. She then grabs hold of the sides of the clock she's sitting on. "Like this." She winks.

"Ben!" Chuck calls out. "Tell us a joke!"

Ben is almost laughing before he even speaks, but he composes himself. "Did I ever tell you guys about the time I tried to organize a professional hide-and-seek tournament? It was a complete failure." He stops and waits.

"Why was it a failure, Ben?" Eve asks. She, too, is starting to laugh.

"Because good hide-and-seek players are hard to find," Ben says.

No one says anything, but then suddenly there's an eruption of laughter.

"Get it?" Ben says. "Hard to find?"

You look around and you realize everyone's clocks are now floating a few inches above the floor. What's more, the ceiling seems to have disappeared completely.

"What sound does a nut make when it sneezes?" Eve yells. She is laughing heartily and her clock is a good three feet off the ground now.

"I know this one!" Emma says. "Cashew!" With a jolt, her clock rises up. She leans over toward you and her clock moves in your direction. "You steer by leaning," she says. "Just don't fall off!"

"Don't what?" you say as Emma zips away. You look down and realize your clock is now a good five feet above ground and the floor beneath you has transformed into thick piles of foam cushions. You grab the sides of the clock and hold on tight.

Now everyone is tossing jokes back and forth, and the clocks they're sitting on are flying all around the room. You cannot stop laughing and you want this never to end.

"Why do ghosts love elevators?" Chuck calls out, then he answers himself: "Because it lifts their spirits!" With both hands securely holding his clock, he maneuvers himself into a flying loop, and then straight up toward the sky, before diving back down again.

The seven of you fly around, laughing and telling jokes, for what feels like hours. By the time you quit, your entire body hurts from laughing. Tears of laughter are streaming down your face. You're exhausted. But you're all still in the air.

"How do we get down?" you ask, wiping at your eyes.

"Easy!" Chuck says. "We jump!"

"Wait!" Eve says. She stares at the floor a bit, and then suddenly an additional three-foot layer of cushioning materializes. "Just to be safe. We're up higher than usual," she explained.

Chuck gives here a salute. "Thank you, ma'am," he says, and then he stands on his clock and jumps down.

"No diving!" Emma tells you. "Not until you're used to it."

You nod and watch as the others all jump off their clocks. Carefully, you climb up to stand on your own clock. Looking down you realize you are very far up, indeed. "Here I come!" you say. You close your eyes and plug your nose and jump.

When you land, you sink into the cushions so far you wonder how you'll ever climb out. It feels like landing in the softest marshmallow, without being sticky. Finally the foam reverses itself and pushes you back to the surface.

"That was amazing," you say to the others, exhausted from laughing. "I haven't laughed that hard in ... well, ever. Speaking of time, I need to get home, but can I come and do this again?"

"Anytime," Chuck says. "Just be sure to bring some jokes!"

You spend the next month coming back to fly in the Experimental Building every day. Years from now you will still remember it as the best time of your life.

THE END

You look at the wall again. The wall that looks to everyone else like a wall, but to you, sometimes, like right now, looks like a door.

"Why can only I see it?" you say, half under your breath. "Are you sure I'm ready?"

Emma lifts a shoulder. "We could ask Dr. Waldo," she says quietly.

You shake your head slowly. "No," you say. "I'm going in."

"You'll probably need us to come with you, right?" says Chuck, eagerly edging closer to you.

"The Two Charlies Guiding Service, here to help," says Charlie. "Two Charlies for the price of one!"

"There's a fee?" you ask, but you're not really paying attention. The door that no one else can see has slid open and now you can see beyond it.

"Well, we can negotiate," says Charlie.

You walk to the doorway. You can feel something inside you pulling you toward the other side. "It's open now. I'm going in," you say.

You step through the doorway. Instantly, the door slams shut behind you.

"Wait—" you say, but it's too late.

Your heart beats fast.

Should you continue on? Or try to get back to the others?

If you continue your adventure, turn to page 107.
If you try to return, turn to page 116.

"I trust you," you say to Ree. "Whatever you think is best." Anything she knows is infinitely more than you do.

"Okay," says Ree. She sighs a heavy sigh of resolve. "I'll take us directly there rather than going through the Hub. The less we potentially interact with you here, the better." She pulls a small sphere out of her pocket, and then loops one arm through your elbow. "Hang on," she says.

Before you have a chance to think twice, she swipes a finger across the sphere and your entire body feels like it's disintegrating. How you're supposed to hold on to her when your cells are breaking apart, you're not sure, but soon it becomes a moot point as you can't differentiate your body from the rest of the universe: there is no need to "hang on," because you and Ree and everything else in the multiverse are one and the same. It's a floating, freeing feeling, and when it quickly starts to dissipate you wish you could hang on to that feeling a little longer. But soon you and Ree are fully intact again, back inside the lighthouse of the lobby.

"What just happened?! And where do I get one of those?" you say, pointing at the sphere in Ree's hand, once your brain seems to be reassembled.

Ree laughs. "We traveled through space, and took you back to your original timeline. I hope. And you get one of these in the Hub," she says. "I don't think they sell them in stores here."

You nod, and there's an awkward silence. "So, I'll see you again?" you say. You want to go right back into the Hub, but you're not sure that's allowed.

"I hope so," Ree says. "You know where to find us!" She walks back into the storage closet, and disappears.

The next day, after a good sleep and a lot of thinking, you return. You can't wait to visit the Hub again. Knowing that it exists is the most amazing discovery you've ever made.

When you get to the lighthouse, though, you're confused. The storage closet is no longer there. Instead, where there once was a door, now there's just a smooth, seamless wall.

You run your hand over the wall, knocking, searching for a hidden way in. "I know it was here," you mumble. "I didn't just dream that." But try as you might, the wall will not yield.

The most amazing discovery you will ever make is now hidden from you, for the rest of time.

THE END

Even though you're a little scared, even though this is new, you decide you can trust yourself in your ability to face whatever comes your way. You want to continue. This door opened only for you, and you are curious what's inside.

You tap on the wall behind you. "I'll be back," you whisper.

You look around, assess your new surroundings. The space is eerily quiet, and it is empty.

You notice a slight glow in the distance. You squint. Is that another door? You walk toward it until it becomes clear that it is indeed a door, glowing a warm, bright yellow.

You hear a click far behind you. You look back, and you realize the door you entered through is open again. You can see Emma waving at you frantically.

You turn back. Next to the glowing yellow door, there is now a glowing red door. Your hair stands up on your neck. Something about that door feels dangerous. But then as you watch, the door shifts from red to a rich orange, a deep yellow, and an earthy green, through the rainbow before settling on a deep, calming midnight blue.

If you open the glowing yellow door, turn to page 108.
If you open the midnight blue door, turn to page 120.
If you go back to where the others are waiting for you, turn to page 127.

The warmth of the yellow door is irresistible. Something inside you tells you this is the door that was meant for you.

The comforting scent of old books rushes at you as you open the door. Inside you find a large library room, the kind of home library a person in a mansion might have. Shelves of books with spines of every width and color line the walls from the floor to the high ceilings, and a wheeled ladder is attached to a railing midway up the wall, allowing access to the higher shelves. Straight ahead of you, a large window looks out over a vast, well-trimmed lawn. A half dozen mallard ducks are swimming in a tranquil lake, and wispy clouds dot the bright blue sky.

Sitting in a rocking chair, looking out over the scene, is a very old woman who somehow also looks very young. Her hair is pure white, white as the clouds, and her skin is wrinkled at the corners of her eyes and lips, like she has spent the last hundred years smiling and laughing. But when she turns to look at you, her eyes are bright and clear.

"You've found it," she says. "Good on you. You've found it."

You approach her and can't help but smile in return.

"What exactly have I found?" you say. You hear a soft whisper—no, dozens of whispers. Barely audible, but you're sure of it. You almost think it's the books, talking to you, calling to you.

"Your own personal magic library," the woman says.

"Magic library?" you say. Your heart flutters with excitement. Whatever a magic library is, it certainly has to be good.

"Indeed," says the woman. "Your reward for your courage, and for trusting your heart."

You stare at her.

She can read your mind, apparently. "Courage," she clarifies, "because you followed your own path. You were willing to take the chance on entering the doorway that was meant for you, even if it meant leaving the others behind." She pauses. "And trusting your heart, because you knew which door was right for you. The warm yellow door that was simple, or the door that seemed dangerous at first but then changed to make you think it was safe? You knew the right choice and you didn't waver. And so here, your reward, is the magic library."

You flush with pleasure, and a bit of relief.

"But what is the magic library?" you ask. "What are all these books?"

"These books," she says, "are everything. There are books with stories you can jump right into, experience as if you were a part of them. And there are books full of empty pages. Write your own stories, and then the magic library will allow you to enter the stories, to live them. All from here, the safety of the library. And when you are done for the day, you will return to the outside world and no time will have passed."

You gasp. "The characters ... they'll be real? I can interact with them?"

The woman's eyes sparkle even brighter. "Yes, yes indeed! Any person, any time, any place. This library was created just for you. By you. It knows your soul. This library will take you anywhere."

"It's like a portal to all the universes," you whisper in awe as you gaze on all the books. Can you ever possibly make it through all of them? You make it your mission to try.

You scan the books until you find one about buried treasure. You open it.

"What do I do?" you ask. "How does it work?"

The woman stands. "Sit here, in this chair," she says, gesturing to the rocking chair. "Start reading. Once you've lost yourself in the story, you won't have to do anything. You will be there." She nods. "And now, I must say goodbye." Without even giving you a chance to thank her, she disappears into the air.

You sit in the rocking chair and start to read. Soon, the characters are alive in your head. You look up and the scene before you is gone. The lawn, the lake, the ducks, all of it has been replaced, and you are now on an island. The sandy beach goes on forever, met in front of you by the turquoise waters of the ocean. In your hands you are now holding an ancient, weathered map.

You stand, turn inland, and start your search for treasure.

THE END

"Can't we just do it here?" you ask. What could go wrong?

Ree hesitates. "Well, I suppose we could." She sounds very uncertain.

But you don't want to leave. What if you can't get back? This place is amazing and you want to explore every corner.

"Yes, let's, please," you say.

Ree inhales deeply, then sighs. "Okay," she says. She reaches for your hand, then closes her eyes, concentrating hard. In a moment, you start to feel like you're being pulled, back, back, back, tight like a rubber band. The pressure builds and builds until you almost can't stand it, and then, suddenly, the pressure is gone.

You look around.

"Did it work?" you ask.

Ree checks her iPert. "I think so," she says. "We'll just have to—"

A shimmer in the room distracts both of you. You feel a pressure again, but this time it feels more like you're being pushed. You take a step forward and turn to see if someone was behind you, but there's no one there. Then, the shimmer grows darker, solidifying, until there, standing before you, right where you just were … is you.

"Um," you say.

"Um," the other you says back.

"Ah, darn it!" Ree says. "Argh!"

"Um, what happened?" you say.

"I knew it was risky doing it here," is all Ree can say. "Let's go."

Without checking to see if you and the other you are following her, she leaves the room, heading back down the hall toward the others.

When they see you, they all cheer for a moment … until they see the second you.

"Well," says Chuck, punching Charlie in the arm lightly. "This is familiar. Did you find another you from another Earth?"

Ree shakes her head, clearly frustrated. "No. I wasn't sure what to do, and I messed up. This is our friend, but from a different timeline, and now they're both here. They're both in our Now." She sighs.

"We need Dr. Waldo," Emma says. "Come on."

As you walk, you follow the other you, fascinated by what you look like from the back. Your hair has a light spot you'd never noticed before. And you decide you really need to work on your posture.

When Dr. Waldo sees you, and the other you, he jumps to the same conclusion Chuck did. "Did you go to another Earth, then, children?" he says with delight. "Always wonderful to meet ourselves!"

"No," says Ree, blushing. "Another time. Same person from nine seconds in the future. I messed up."

"Ah, well, my dear, no worries, I see, no worries, no worries. There are no mistakes, just learning opportunities." He looks you up and down, then does the same with the other you. "Well, and you see, you're not the first to make this error at any rate. We already know the consequences of this one." He nods slowly, looking at the other you. "Yes, yes," he says. "I'm afraid so."

"Afraid so, what?" the other you says. "What are you afraid of?"

"Well," Dr. Waldo says. "What we learned the last time this happened is that while you can both be here in the Hub, the Hub won't let you both out at the same time. We don't know why, really, but ..."

"Wait," says Ben. "Is that why there used to be one Howard in the lab, and now there are two? Did this happen to Howard?"

Dr. Waldo shrugs. "Yes, yes, well, you see, that's confidential, can't comment on that. But he's an excellent scientist. Having two Howards around is quite an advantage, you see. A definite advantage."

You and the other you, however, are not paying much attention. You know what you're thinking, and you're the one to say it: "So one of us has to stay here for the rest of our lives?"

Dr. Waldo tilts his head. "Well, that, or you can alternate. It's up to you, really. The main thing is that one of you always must be here."

"And if we both leave?" you ask. "What happens then?"

Dr. Waldo shrugs. "Well, from what we can tell, until we figure out another solution ... you can't both leave."

"But what if we do?" you ask again. "What happens?"

"You literally cannot," Dr. Waldo says. "The Hub won't let you both out at the same time."

You feel a chill, and you lock eyes with the other you, who is from a timeline either nine seconds before or after yours; you can't quite get it straight.

"I suppose there are worse places to be stuck," the other you says. "Maybe we can trade off."

You think of all the people at home, all your friends, everything in your normal life. "You know what, for now, I'll stay here. You go explore. And when you're ready, we'll switch."

The other you nods. "I'll come back. I promise."

The other you goes off, back to Earth, while you explore the Hub. Days pass, then months, then years. Either the other you forgot, or chose not to return. You become one of the greatest scientists in the Hub. Still, although the Hub is infinite, you start to feel slightly trapped.

Then one day, when he is quite old, the other you returns.

"It's you," you say.

"Is it really you?" the other you says.

You size each other up. The years have not been easy on the other you. The other you looks old and tired, and is wearing glasses. You, however, living in a place where everything is possible, have invented ways to stay young. Years ago your eyesight started to dim, but you cured your eyes. Once you got a bit older you worked on reversing your age, and now you are young again.

"Time was good to you," the other you says.

"And now it's my turn to go live out my life," you say.

The other you nods.

"I have a cabin over there," you say, pointing to a wooded area in the distance, past a river you created, next to a mountain you imagined into existence. "It's yours now."

You are beyond excited. You can't even believe this is happening. This is the moment you've been waiting for. Without even saying goodbye to the others living and working in the Hub, you race back to the elevator and make your way into the lighthouse.

It looks the same, only a little the worse for wear.

You step outside and breathe in the fresh air. Maybe fifty years have passed, but you are as spry as ever.

It's time for your life to begin.

THE END

Your sense of panic increases. You're letting the panic overwhelm you but you don't try to stop it. You're in over your head, and you know it.

You knock on the wall. "Hey!" you call out. "Help me!"

You close your eyes to try to enhance your other senses, but you hear nothing. No Emma, Eve, Chuck, Ben, or any of the others responding to your plea.

You are alone.

A voice inside your head tells you to believe, to trust yourself, that you are safe and have what you need, but you mentally bat that voice away. This is too much. Too far outside your comfort zone. You want to go home.

You sit down on the floor, hugging your knees to your chest. You close your eyes and try to breathe slowly.

"I want to go home," you say out loud. "I want to go back to Earth."

Your eyes are still closed but suddenly from behind your eyelids you sense that the light in the room has changed. The smell, too—there was no scent before but now your nose is detecting fresh cut grass. Nearby, a bird chirps, and then you hear the call of a seagull farther in the distance. A wave crashes against a shore.

You open your eyes.

You are back at the lighthouse, sitting outside in the grass. The sun is beaming down on you. Wispy clouds float in a bright blue sky. You are safe.

"But wait—" you say, and you run inside the lighthouse, into the lobby, to the storage room door. You knock on it, but nothing happens. No one comes.

"Emma!" you call. "Ben!"

Silence.

You wave at the door, in case there's a camera or something they might see, but still no one comes. You try the door knob, but it is locked and will not turn.

You wander around room, knocking on walls. You stand on a bench to try to tap at the ceiling. You run up the stairs of the lighthouse tower.

There is nothing there. There is no portal. There is no other universe.

A voice comes into your head. "You should have trusted yourself," it says. You sigh. You knew—instinctively you knew, back inside that room—that everything would be okay, but you let your fears stop you. And now your chance is gone.

With one last knock on the storage room door, you sigh again, and then you start walking down the path toward toward your cabin.

THE END

You have no idea what to do. You're scared that if you try to make yourself big again, you'll mess it up even further. Your only hope is that the others might somehow have had some experience with this.

"Of course they do," you mumble to yourself. "Who hasn't accidentally shrunk themselves down to smaller than a grain of sand?"

With a deep sigh, you turn and run toward the edge of the table, where the shadows have been moving around. You can't believe how far it is. If only you could fly …

Then you remember. You're still in the Hub, as far as you know. This is a place where everything is possible, they told you. They told you more than once. They hammered it into your brain.

So maybe … maybe you could fly. Even if you are less than a millimeter tall.

You stop, panting from the running. You close your eyes and concentrate hard. You have wings, you tell yourself, imagining them sprouting from your back … no, no, you think, what happens if you get wings but can't get rid of them once you're full size again? You open your eyes and shake your head. "Focus," you tell yourself. You close your eyes and think. You can control the atoms of the air, yes, that's it. The atoms of the air will lift and carry you wherever you want to go. You imagine all the molecules of air holding you up and passing you forward as if you were in some mosh pit. Not quite flying. More like surfing. Definitions aside, though, you can feel it happening: you are being lifted into the air by the air molecules themselves. You think hard about where you want to go. Opening your eyes, you see it happening. "Faster" you whisper, and instantaneously you are flying though the air toward the outside of the table.

"STOP!" you say when you reach the edge. You're not sure exactly how you're controlling this phenomenon, but you decide now is not the time to question it.

You tip your head backward to look up at the others, who are now giants. Mountains. Planets. How in the world will you get their attention?

Everything is possible, you think. You just need to get creative.

Two ideas jump to mind: using the power of your mind again you could create either a giant megaphone that you can speak into, or a banner with your message.

If you create a megaphone, turn to page 140.
If you create a banner, turn to page 150.

The yellow door seems like a good, solid choice. But the color-changing door seems more interesting.

For a second you feel a flash of doubt in your mind, but you dismiss it. After all, what could go wrong? You want to push yourself out of your comfort zone.

As you reach for the doorknob for the door that is now midnight blue, a rush of electricity almost pushes your hand away before it subsides. Not wanting to give the electric surge a chance to return, you quickly grab the doorknob and turn it.

Darkness instantly engulfs you. You can't see an inch in front of your face. You hold up your hand to your nose but can't see it at all.

You take a step forward. Then another.

On the third step you realize too late that there is no floor beneath your foot. You are falling. You fall and you fall and you fall for what seems like minutes, hours, forever. You wonder if you will ever stop falling.

Until finally, you do.

You don't land, really; rather, it seems that suddenly, the floor reappears, and you are standing on it. There is no jolt of impact, no crashing into the ground, just a reappearance of solid footing.

"Huh," you say. The space around you is still pitch black. You reach out your hands and shuffle around, keeping your feet on the floor so you don't step again into nothingness.

After a while, the darkness begins to fade away. Slowly at first, so you're not sure if you're just imagining it, but then the blackness around you turn to charcoal and the charcoal turns to gray, and you're able to see your hand in front of your face again. The fog lifts entirely and you find yourself in a pure white room. There's nothing in the room except a pure white desk, and a man sitting at it. His hair is white, his skin is wrinkled, and he is watching you.

"Hello?" you say hesitantly. He doesn't look mean, but also he doesn't look friendly.

"You didn't listen," he says.

"I'm so sorry," you say. "It's not that I didn't listen; I just couldn't hear you before. I'm listening now?"

He shakes his head. "No. You didn't listen to yourself," he says.

You are starting to feel uncomfortable. "I didn't listen to myself?" you say.

"The door," he says. "You let yourself be deceived by the fancy looks. You knew better. You didn't listen to your heart."

You want to object, but you know it's true. "But is that so wrong? I was … I was outside my comfort zone. I was taking a risk."

"There's a difference between taking a risk and ignoring your instincts," he says. "Yes, we must step outside our comfort zones. That's how we grow. But also we must learn to know when we are acting—or not acting—out of fear, and when we are being rash. We must learn bravery, not bravado. Confidence, not cockiness. There is a difference. You must learn to trust your instincts, and you must gain enough wisdom that your instincts are trustworthy."

You aren't sure how to respond.

"We made a mistake," he says. "We thought you were ready but you still have much to learn. Go home and think on it. When you are ready, you may return, and try again. Until then, the lighthouse will be closed to you."

"Wait!" you call out, but already the room has changed. The white room is gone, the man is gone, and you find yourself at the lighthouse, outside on the doorstep.

You try to open the door, but it is locked. You knock, you pound on the door for several minutes, but no one comes.

You turn and head down the path away from the lighthouse. "Bravery, not bravado," you say to yourself, and as you walk back to your cabin, you think deeply, trying to figure out the difference.

THE END

It's an interesting situation you find yourself in, indeed. You are minuscule, but also you seem to be fully functioning. Your thoughts feel just as large as they were when you were full-sized.

What's more, no one can stop you now.

Whereas before the table made for cramped quarters as a portal, now it's practically the size of a space ship, relative to you.

And if you can figure out how to make a portal, surely you can figure out how to steer this thing.

You can hear rumbles and murmurs from the others, but you're so small that it sounds like low thunder. Indistinct. You can't make out the words but you imagine—or at least hope—they're wondering where you went.

Regardless, they can't hear you. You yell a few times to test the theory and get no response.

Time to fly this table, you decide.

You decide that if you're going to go hurtling through the universes inside of a table, you'd like it to be fully enclosed. You close your eyes and take three deep breaths, then you put all your focus into imagining that the two open sides of the cube are now sealed tight. With a door, you think at the last minute. A door for you to use so you aren't stuck inside.

You picture the new walls—towering, now, so high above your head—you picture them being made of the same strong, reflective material of the other sides. While you're at it, you imagine recessed lights in the top of the cube, so you can see, and a panel on one wall that you can use to set coordinates. You wonder briefly how it will work, but then instinctively you decide: you will set your hand on a panel, and imagine where you want to go, and the portal will take you there.

At the last minute, you decide to make your quarters more comfortable. You imagine multiple levels inside the table, like a house with several floors. Though you can't see through the walls and floors that have now appeared, you put your full faith into knowing that everything is being imagined into existence exactly as you are creating it in your mind. Lots of overhead lights. A bedroom with an enormous, cozy bed. A bathroom with a jacuzzi tub. A living room with comfortable couches and chairs and plenty of books to read. A fully stocked kitchen, in case there's no food wherever you land. And in the basement, where you are now, a replicator, which can be used to create whatever else you need.

You feel all of this inside your mind deeply, calmly, like you're remembering it rather than imagining it. You've been here before. You've seen all this before. You aren't making it up but rather recalling it. And when you open your eyes again …

There it all is. Exactly as you imagined it.

You smile. *Everything is possible*, you think.

There's an anticipation in the air, like the table—rather, your personal spaceship—is listening, waiting for your command.

It's a whisper on the air. *Where to? Where to?*

If you decide to travel to a parallel Earth, turn to page 137.
If you decide to let the portal be the guide, turn to page 153.

Nothing has changed. You are still lost in the infinite darkness.

You try again. Once more. One more time. But every time, you return to the middle of nothingness.

You are caught in an infinite loop.

Turn to page 125.

You look around.

You are still in the Hub.

The others are still staring at you.

"Back so soon?" says Charlie.

"Charlie, be nice," says Emma.

"Hey, it's possible. A person can leave and have a whole adventure and come back at the same time they left. We've seen it happen," Charlie says.

"I know, but…" Emma says, shushing her brother.

"Did it work?" says Eve graciously. "Did you go somewhere?"

You shake your head sheepishly and climb out of the table. You rub your left leg, which has developed a bit of a cramp.

"So," says Ree, smiling. She loops an arm through yours. "Shall we show you around then?"

You nod. "Let's go," you say.

THE END

The choices make you nervous. You just discovered that there's more than one universe, and that people can travel between universes, and now they want you to pick a door? You decide maybe you're not ready for any doors. This is a bit more than you were prepared to deal with today. You walk back toward the hallway and you wonder if they're going to think you're a coward. You sort of wish you were invisible.

When you reach the doorway, Emma is still there waving at you.

"Well, that was a waste of time, I guess," you say with a weak laugh.

But no one seems to hear you.

You walk past them into the hallway, but no one turns. They are still looking through the doorway and waving.

"You guys," you say. "I'm over here." You're starting to panic a bit. "Can't you see me?"

"You're back!" Emma says, and you feel a bit of relief until you realize she's not looking at you.

"What do you mean a waste of time?" Eve says, still looking to the doorway.

A shiver goes through you. Are they responding to your words from several seconds ago?

"Guys," you say. "Something weird is going on."

They all turn and look at you.

"Of course we can see you," Ben says. "Why would you think we can't see you?"

You blink. They are definitely a few seconds behind you in time. You are going to have to talk, and also keep your previous words in mind so you know what they're replying to. What was the last thing you said?

You've stood there long enough, though, that now they've heard your last statement.

"What do you mean, something weird is going on?" says Charlie. He looks back to the dark room you were in. "Did something happen in there?"

They stare at you and you realize it has been a very long time since you spoke, and that time will seem even longer to them.

"I'm … I think I'm ahead of you in time, or something," you say, shaking your head in disbelief. "I'm speaking, and it's taking a few seconds before you hear me. I'm standing here watching you react to what I said several seconds ago."

"Hello?" says Chuck. "Cat got your tongue?"

You remember the long silence. Soon they'll hear what you said and will get caught up. You just keep talking.

"I'm ahead of you in time," you repeat. "That's why it seems like I'm just standing here. We're … out of phase or something. Not by a lot." You pause. "Do you know what to do?"

You stop and wait for the others to catch up.

"You're out of phase?" Chuck says finally. He looks at his sister. "Ree? Sounds like this one's for you."

You have no idea what that means, but you're glad they're on the case.

Ree frowns. "That's tricky. I'll need to know exactly how much in the future you are," she says to you. "Do you have a … no, even if you do it probably doesn't work here," she says, mumbling, answering herself. She pulls a device out of her pocket. "iPert," she explains. "Our version of a phone." She taps on the screen for a few seconds. "Okay, it's on the stopwatch. I'm going to set it down so you can pick it up. I think that will work?"

Before she sets the iPert down, you see it on the floor. Your mind twists, trying to figure this out, but you just pick up the device.

Ree looks at you. "Okay. You start the stopwatch, and when you start it, say 'NOW.' When we hear you, we'll say 'STOP.' The time between those two, hopefully, is how far you are in the future." She squints. She doesn't look too sure that this will work, but you have no ideas of your own.

"Okay," you say. Rather than waiting for them to hear your confirmation, you just start. As you tap the stopwatch you call out "NOW!"

The seconds tick by … one … two … three … four … five … six … seven … eight … nine …

"STOP" yell all the others.

You stop the stopwatch and hold it up. "About nine seconds," you say.

Another nine seconds later, Ree nods. "Okay."

You have no idea what's going on, but you decide to trust her.

"You can do just nine seconds?" Chuck says.

"Yeah," Ree says, "I think so. But … I don't want to mix up timelines and meet myself. That just gets messy." She looks at you. "Let's go down to the Head in the

Clouds room." She starts down the hallway, then turns. "I can't figure out if you're already with me or ahead of me or behind me? Regardless, it's that room. Meet me inside."

You follow her direction and see a door with a cloud-shaped sign over it that says "Head in the Clouds."

You enter the room and notice a lovely peaceful smell. It calms you. The room is neither bright nor dim but rather just comfortably light, with sparkling lights around the baseboard and the ceiling. Soft instrumental music is playing, and a thick rug covers the floor, with several smaller rugs scattered on top. You're curious about this room, but mostly you want to get back to your timeline.

Ree is at your side. "Okay, I'm jumping ahead now," she says. She closes her eyes and seems to focus, but you have no idea what's happening. Then there's a slight energy shift in the room, and she opens her eyes.

"Time travel," she says, smiling. "It's kind of my thing. I figured it would be easier to talk this way."

"Wait, we're in sync now?" you say, incredulous. "You're in my … uh, my time zone? You … you time traveled?"

She replies immediately, so you know the answer. "Yup," she says, as if it's the most normal thing in the world. In the universes. "Now. What happened?"

"I don't know," you say, shrugging helplessly. "I went through that door in the hall and then when I tried to come back, I was in the future."

"Hmm," Ree says. "Okay." She pauses, and you can see

the wheels turning in her head. "Here's the thing," she says finally. "Time is tricky. And there are infinite time-lines and infinite yous, even just nine seconds apart. We don't know why you skipped forward in time, so we don't actually know whether this you is a future you or the you from our timeline in the future. So if I take you back in the Hub, I'm not sure whether there will be two of you or if I'll leave the current timeline without you. My gut is telling me I should take you back in time on Earth, at the lighthouse. I can't really explain it, but that seems right. But it's up to you. Do you want to go back in time here in the Hub? Or on Earth?"

You stare at her. You're not entirely sure what she just said. Still, she is waiting for an answer.

If you trust Ree's gut and go back in time on Earth, turn to page 105.

If you want to go back in time in the Hub, turn to page 111.

Your gut tells you that you can do this. Without saying anything to the others, you close your eyes and start to concentrate. In your mind's eye you see the table you created, just as vividly as you saw it when you were imagining it, and just as vividly as when you saw it before you in real life. You picture its edges and textures. You imagine the feel of it as your fingertips trace the surface. You can almost feel the weight of it inside your mind.

Then, you imagine it all fading away, the atoms and molecules of the table breaking apart and dissolving into thin air. Though your eyes are still shut tight, you can almost feel the table disappearing. A gentle breeze blows past your face, and you smile.

You continue to focus on the table until in your mind the entire thing is completely gone. A corner of your lip lifts as you recall Chuck and Charlie bemoaning their fate on a planet of quicksand. Amateurs, you think. Some people are made for this sort of thing, and maybe, well, who are you to say anything bad about a couple of nice people you just met? But maybe not everyone is cut out for this sort of thing.

You think you hear one of the others calling your name, but they sound so distant. You're that focused, you think, so focused that even sound isn't penetrating your train of thought.

You nod slightly, to yourself. The table is gone. You're sure of it. You can just tell. It is no longer anywhere near you.

You open your eyes to discover you're right.

The table is nowhere near you.

But also: neither are any of the others.

You are no longer in the Hub.

You have no idea where you are.

You look down and realize you are not standing on firm ground. The land, as far as you can see around you, is made up of sand.

Quicksand. Or more accurately, slow sand.

And you are very slowly sinking.

Or are you?

Suddenly it occurs to you: maybe none of this is real. Maybe all of this is in your mind. You thought your way into this position. Maybe you can think your way out.

If you try to think yourself out, turn to page 135.

If you try to climb out, turn to page 142.

You laugh. "It's an interesting thing, hearing people's thoughts. Honestly, it's not all it's cracked up to be. But one thing I know for sure is how badly you want to study me. Your thoughts are so powerful that I can feel how you're feeling. You're beyond excited about the possibilities and that's making me excited, too."

Dr. Waldo's burst of joy is so strong that when he starts dancing a jig out of delight, you start dancing with him.

"Excellent! Excellent!" he says. Then he pauses and concentrates. You know he's imagining a house into existence for you, but you let him reveal his surprise. After a moment, he speaks again. "I've just created a quiet house for you to live in while you're here. I'll transport you straight there so you don't have to face all the noise unless you want to."

He transports you to the home he created inside the Hub. It's small but comfortable, and you know you can make—with the power of your mind—changes that will make you happy. Within a day he has come up with a plan of study, and you stay in the Hub, working with him to understand your mind. Eventually you learn to turn the ability on and off, and you go on to become one of the Hub's most legendary scientists.

THE END

You decide to try to think your way out. This is all an illusion, anyway, right? Even the Hub is probably an illusion. In fact, it's probably more of a dream rather than an illusion.

Your mind starts to spiral. You start to question all of reality. Are you real? If you're asking whether you're real is that proof that you're real? Could you ask yourself if you were real, from within a dream? Is the Hub real? Are you just asleep? Are you asleep in the Hub or asleep in your bed?

You feel yourself sinking lower into the sand. Slowly, slowly, but surely. You are up to your knees now.

Spread out, you think. Spread out and swim.

You're not sure where the idea comes from but you try it anyway. You lean back, trying to kick your legs up as you do so, but you can't pull them out of the sand. Now your back is sinking into the sand as well.

"Think!" you yell at yourself as you feel the sand making its way up your sides and neck. You imagine yourself back in the Hub. You think about Dr. Waldo and the Charlies and Emma and Ree and the space where you created the table.

Your mind is swirling, though, and you can't focus. You start to worry about what will happen if you sink so far that you can't breathe. You inhale deeply. You can still breathe.

"Think!" you yell.

You imagine yourself anywhere. Anywhere but here. You are lying in bed. You are not sinking in sand but rather you are just cozy in your bed, asleep, having the strangest dream of your life.

You feel the sand start to cover your face. You close your eyes. Everything goes dark.

"Think!" you yell inside your head.

Suddenly, you are sputtering for breath. You sit up. At first you see no light at all, but then your eyes adjust and you see a thin line of brightness. You reach toward it and your hands encounter something. A curtain. You pull the curtain aside to reveal a window.

It is the window in your bedroom.

You are in your bed.

You sit up, breathing hard.

You look around you. Nothing has changed from when you were last here.

Did any of that just happen?

Or was it all a dream?

THE END

The idea of a parallel Earth has intrigued you since the moment you first heard of it. The idea of seeing a parallel Earth is interesting, sure, but even more than that, who could resist the opportunity to meet the parallel version of themselves?

You decide now is your chance.

You walk to the control panel you created and place your palm flat against it. You close your eyes and—

And you realize you don't actually know how portals work. To get to the Hub, you walked into a lighthouse, then walked into the Hub.

You tilt your head. This may be more complicated than you thought.

You shrug. You managed to turn the table into a spaceship. Undoubtedly you can get this thing to travel to a parallel Earth.

"Undoubtedly," you repeat, this time out loud. Because you're certain that certainty is required. If you have a moment of doubt when you're in the middle of traveling, if you let your mind wander for a second to, say, the middle of a ferocious fight between two Tyrannosaurus rexes—

Rexes? Is that right? You wonder. Rexi? What is the plural of rex?

You shudder involuntarily. If you can't keep focused on an idea then you might actually end up in a T-rex fight, and that would not be good.

Although, you think, with you at the size you're at now, they might not even notice you.

"Focus," you say to yourself.

You close your eyes again and start to focus. "Don't think about dinosaurs," you whisper to yourself. Then you start to think about a parallel Earth. You imagine it looking exactly like your own Earth but with a few variations. You picture the house you live in, but with different furniture. You imagine yourself out in front, getting ready to go for a walk around the neighborhood. You imagine meeting yourself …

Wait, you think. Will you be your full size? Or this tiny size?

Full size, of course, you decide. You imagine yourself full size, meeting a parallel you on this parallel Earth.

A parallel Earth wouldn't have dinosaurs in the same timeline you're alive in, would it? Things couldn't get that off track?

"Focus," you whisper to yourself. You think about you and your parallel self seeing each other for the first time. Your jaws drop open and you look around to see if you're being filmed, but no, this is real. You punch each other on the shoulder then give a hug, then you start talking and don't stop until the sun goes down. After the sun goes down. You become best friends and visit each other all the time.

You feel this so intensely that you know it's real. You feel a slight breeze, which suggests that you're not where you were a few moments ago—you're no longer in the Hub. You have traveled. Somewhere.

You open your eyes.

If you think you focused well enough, turn to page 171.
If you think maybe you got distracted for a second, turn to page 174.

A megaphone, you decide. You close your eyes and start to imagine it. What does a megaphone even look like? You can suddenly only imagine cartoon megaphones. Clip art. You think there's a button of some kind, something you press. You imagine a giant funnel with a button. No, you think, that's not specific enough. You start to sweat. You look at your arm and it occurs to you that if you're the size of an atom, the sweat on your arm must be absolutely microscopic.

"Stop," you say to yourself. "Focus."

How big would a normal size drop of sweat be, in comparison to how big you are now? You can't help but wonder.

"FOCUS," you shout. You wonder if the others could hear you at all.

"Megaphone," you say. You close your eyes again but wipe a drop of sweat from your brow. Again you wonder about the size of a drop of water. It would be bigger than you, definitely. But how big?

Suddenly you feel drenched in sweat. You open your eyes and realize you are surrounded by water. Are you in a pool? You push off from the ground and try to swim, but which way should you go? The water seems to be self-contained. No walls holding it in.

"A drop of sweat," you think, moaning in your mind. You didn't will a megaphone into existence. You created a drop of sweat.

You keep swimming, holding your breath, your lungs about to burst. Finally you reach the side of the water drop. You push, but with nothing to leverage yourself against, the surface tension of the drop of water is too high. You push again but only manage to push yourself back toward the inside of the drop. You can't hold your breath much longer. You start to get dizzy.

And then everything goes blank. Your story is over.

THE END

You shake your head, resigned to the facts. However you got yourself into this mess, the results are very real. You can't think yourself out. You have to act.

Somewhere in the back of your mind you recall having seen something about quicksand on an old TV show.

"Spread out. Swim." The thought comes into your mind from nowhere but you trust it. You maneuver yourself so that you're lying on your stomach, stretching out your arms and legs as far as you can. Then you slowly start swim-crawling forward. You can't tell for sure, but the ground looks a little more firm off to your right, so you head in that direction. After a few yards, you can tell the ground beneath you is getting more firm, so you keep going until you're sure you're on solid ground again.

You brush some dirt from your clothes and look around. You're on a vast, flat plain. What you first thought was quicksand looks different now that you've had a chance to really inspect it. Now, it looks like an endless lake, more than anything else. A lake as far as you can see, and yet it's one you can walk on, with odd, shallow pits and bubbles, craters and ditches. You look down and can almost see yourself reflected back at you.

Directly ahead of you, far in the distance, the sky is darker than it is on either side of you. You turn. The world behind you looks dark as well.

Suddenly a tremendous cloud of darkness fills the sky—but only to the right of you. A thunderous cacophony breaks out, a loud rumbling and rolling sound. You stare at the dark shadow and finally you notice it has edges. The shadow moves left, then right, then another shadow moves in next to it. The second shadow is of a different texture. It looks familiar, somehow.

You feel your heart beating faster.

You squint again and look more closely at the shadows.

That isn't dark clouds. What you're seeing is clothes. And now you remember where you've seen the second shadow before.

That shadow is no shadow. That shadow is Ree's skirt.

Your heart races even faster. You twirl around. In front of you, a dark sky. It expands out to the right where it mirrors the dark shadows that are moving in the air. You feel the breeze of the shadows as you turn to look behind you again. The shadows are reflected there as well.

You have not gone anywhere, you realize.

You have shrunk down to the size of a cell, maybe. Smaller. An atom.

You are inside the table. What you thought was quicksand was just a thin film of dirt.

And no one else knows where you are.

If you try to get the others' attention, turn to page 118.
If you try to use the table as a portal, turn to page 123.
If you try to make yourself big again, turn to page 148.

You close your eyes and steady your breathing. Inhale for four counts, hold for four counts, exhale for four counts, hold for four counts. You focus solely on your breathing and ignore everything that is happening inside your head …

… Which is a lot. As Dr. Waldo taps at the keyboard, you can practically feel all the thoughts linking together like millions of magnets, then being pulled out of your skull like strings. It doesn't hurt, really, but at the same time it's not at all comfortable. You can tell that whatever he's doing, it's working, though: slowly, the noise in your brain is becoming quieter. First Chuck's thoughts disappear, then Charlie's, then Eve's, Ree's, Ben's, and finally Emma's. Last to go are Dr. Waldo's thoughts. And then, you are left alone with nothing but your own thoughts.

"Stop," you whisper. You are exhausted, but you feel calm.

Dr. Waldo's tapping stops.

You continue breathing. Four counts in, hold for four, four counts out, hold for four. The peace is exquisite.

You open your eyes and smile.

"And now," you say, "if you all don't mind, I think I will go home."

THE END

You squint your eyes. While there are not as many thoughts storming through your mind as there were before you entered this room, the number keeps growing.

"Can everyone please stop thinking," you whisper almost under your breath.

They hear you, but it doesn't help. Now you hear them thinking about not thinking. It's like the elephant in the room, Chuck is thinking. Then he thinks about Rupert, Dr. Waldo's two-dimensional elephant. You want to stick with that thought but Emma is very loudly counting sheep in her head, then thinking that maybe sheep are too active and she should count cotton balls. Or do mathematics tables. She starts multiplying in her head. One times one is one …

"PLEASE," you beg Dr. Waldo. "Please do something!"

Dr. Waldo says nothing but you hear him worrying. He has never tried this machine. It was all just hypothetical. He wanted more time, he really needs more time. Maybe he should take you back in time to get you more time?

The elephants in Chuck's brain are now dancing. Chuck is swatting at the thoughts in his head trying to get them to stop but they're only multiplying. Charlie is staring at Chuck and you know Charlie is thinking that Chuck must be thinking something crazy and he needs to stop. Charlie is wondering what Chuck is thinking. Charlie places a bet in his mind that Chuck is thinking about their plans for a trip to see the plassensnare world. Charlie wants to voice this bet but reminds himself to stop thinking.

One times five is five. One times five is six. No. One times six is six. Oh shoot. Emma wonders if she should start over. She's too distracted. She can't think straight.

Ree is counting her breaths. Or trying to, but she is thinking also about Ben. Ben is thinking that he was supposed to help Dr. Waldo test this room but …

"PLEASE!" you say, loudly and firmly. "DO SOMETHING."

You hear Dr. Waldo tapping madly at the computer. At last, you think. At last, he is doing something.

Suddenly you feel an enormous pull, like someone put giant suction cups all over your head. Everything inside your head is being pulled out. All the thoughts. Chuck's, Ben's, all of it. There goes Emma's multiplication tables. There goes Ree's breaths. There goes your own—

—wait—

—your mind—your thoughts—are going too—

—you try to speak, to tell Dr. Waldo to stop, but you have forgotten what words are—

—

—he won't stop—

—

—everything is gone. Everything. Your mind has been removed from your body. It is now floating out in the universe. You look down and see yourself sitting in the chair, but there is no way back, and no way to tell them where you are.

You can see the horror on Dr. Waldo's face as he realizes what he's done, and the terror as the others reach understanding, as well.

But suddenly, you realize you now have no limitations. No boundaries whatsoever. You are everything and everywhere, everywhen, all at once. You close your eyes—you have no eyes, but mentally, you close your eyes—and think about home. You open your eyes, and you are home. Blink, and you are on the moon. Blink, and you are on the other side of the universe. Blink, and you are at the beginning of time. Blink, and you are at the end.

You are one with all of existence. For the rest of eternity, you will float in the expanse of all that is.

THE END

Your heart is beating hard and fast inside you, and for a moment it occurs to you that your heart is now smaller than a speck of dust. The tiniest heart in the universe, maybe.

Something comes hurtling at you through the air, making your heart beat even faster. You duck, screaming, your scream just barely a scratch of a sound to the others.

"What was that?" you cry out after the object, which is now floating away. You blink, and then you realize it was just a dust mote, floating through the air.

You look at your chest. Not only is your heart smaller than a speck of dust; your entire body is.

You feel yourself starting to panic, so you know you need to act fast before you can't think anymore.

"BIG," you think. It is not a sophisticated thought, by any means, but you fill your entire mind, body, and soul with the word. "BIG," you think. "I want to be BIG again."

Next thing you know, you are growing. You are growing so fast that you lose your breath—you can't breathe fast enough to fill your expanding lungs. You cough and sputter, trying to get enough air, and you only barely notice when your body grows so large that you burst through the table, completely breaking it to splinters. But you forgot one thing: to specify exactly HOW big you wanted to grow. You are now twice as tall as everyone else, who you can see watching you with amazement and fear in their eyes. Now you are four times bigger. You keep growing, so fast, you can't breathe—

"NORMAL SIZE!" Your voice booms through the

entire Hub. "NORMAL SIZE!" You fill your brain and body and soul with the thought, and you repeat it out loud over and over and over: "I want to be normal size again. Normal human size. Normal size." The words become a mumbled mantra, but you are shrinking again and your lungs have enough air once again and you begin to sob.

You don't remember falling asleep, but when you wake up, someone somehow has returned you to your own home, your own bed.

You hope it was all a nightmare. You will never return to that lighthouse again.

THE END

You almost have to laugh. It's all so absurd. You feel like you're in a cartoon or a video game, but the reality is, this is your life now. You are tiny and you need to create a giant banner with your message on it.

You plop yourself down on the floor to think. You don't want to use too many words. They're going to be confused. What should the banner say?

Then it just pops into your head: you need a banner that says, "I'M DOWN HERE" with a giant arrow pointing right at you.

You close your eyes and get into a meditative state, blocking out all other thoughts and sounds. You visualize the banner: It is large—by your current standards it is unfathomably enormous, but by your normal human-sized body's standards, you think maybe five feet long by two feet high. You're not sure, but that sounds good, so you put that thought firmly in your mind: A giant banner, five feet long by two feet high. Bright yellow. Lettering in black, reading "I'M DOWN HERE," and a giant red arrow filling up the rest of the space on the banner, and the whole thing floating right above your head, with the very tip of the arrow pointing directly at you.

You let the image form in your mind until it completely consumes you. You are the sign and the sign is you. There is no possibility this sign doesn't exist. You know as sure as you know you're alive, that the sign is floating above your head, with the arrow pointing at you.

Suddenly, all the voices that you've heard as a voluminous murmur go silent. You open your eyes cautiously. Next thing you know, four giant eyes are staring straight at you. Emma and Ben are leaning over, looking in your direction.

"It says here." You can just make out the words; they're so large it's hard for your tiny ears to focus the sound, but you are sure you just heard Ben speak.

"Get a magnifying glass," Emma says, and in an instant she's holding a vast, round piece of glass and angling it in your direction.

"There!" she says excitedly, and she hands the magnifying glass to Ben. "See?"

"Right!" says Ben, staring through the glass at you. You wave. Ben waves back.

"Careful!" you hear Eve say. "We don't want to squish our new friend!"

"What do we do?" says Chuck. "Dr. Waldo! What do we do?"

But even as they are scrambling, Dr. Waldo has started working his magic. You are growing, and somehow you can tell it's through Dr. Waldo's Hub-enabled imagination. With the power of his mind, he is bringing you back to normal size.

As you grow, you crawl out of the table and back onto the floor so you don't have to stoop. First you're as tall as the others' knees, then their waists, then their shoulders, and finally you're back to your own normal height. You feel a sort of shiver as the growing stops.

"That was amazing," says Chuck, his eyes lit up.

"Like, wow," says Charlie. He turns to Chuck and, everyone can tell they're having the same idea: they want to try this, too.

"I don't recommend it," you say. "At least, not without telling someone first."

The yellow sign you created is still hanging over the table, pointing to where you once were.

"That was some good thinking," Emma says, noticing the object of your gaze. "That sign. You're a natural at this."

"Necessity is the mother of invention?" you say. You had to learn quick, so you did.

"Well," says Ben, "regardless, it does seem you have some innate skill. Would you have any interest in joining us on some studies we are working on? We're always looking for some new talent!"

You smile. You feel invigorated, thinking about the possibilities.

"I'd like that," you say. And so, a week later, you're back in the Hub, at work with Ben and Dr. Waldo to discover new properties of the mind and the universes. In a few decades, when Dr. Waldo retires, you become the director of the Hub, spending your time proving that inside this magical space, everything truly is possible.

THE END

You're up for an adventure, and you imagine the portal may have some amazing ideas you couldn't even think about.

"Okay, you're in the driver's seat," you say to the portal. You sit down in a nearby chair.

You sit a while, staring at the walls. Nothing happens. You think maybe you didn't ask in the right way.

"Hey, portal," you say. "Take me somewhere nice, please?"

You sort of wish you had a seatbelt. Will the portal fly fast? How will this work, anyway?

Still, nothing happens. You're starting to wonder what you should do next, but then you notice something changing on the wall in front of you. At first, it looks like the wall is just starting to glow a bit in two spots. Then the glowing areas get brighter and take the form of two buttons: one blue, and one green.

The buttons flash. The portal is asking you to pick one.

If you push the blue button, turn to page 175.
If you push the green button, turn to page 177.

You walk into the quiet room. The others follow. Once they're all inside, Ben shuts the door.

The difference is palpable. Whereas before you were experiencing all the thoughts, emotions, scents, memories, and images from inside the heads of everyone in the Hub, in this room the onslaught has scaled down to just this small group.

It's still too much.

"Can you all leave?" you say. Your tone is sharp, but you're at your wit's end. "Everyone but Dr. Waldo."

Chuck protests. "We just want to help—" he starts.

"If you don't leave, I'll tell everyone everything you're thinking," you say, your eyes locked on his so he knows you're not kidding.

Chuck's mouth snaps shut. He backs up toward the door. "We should all leave," he says, then races out without bothering to see if the others are behind him.

"But—" Emma says.

You raise an eyebrow to her. "I hear everything," you say. "Past and present. And I'm not sure, but maybe even future."

Emma makes a little sound, then hurries out after Chuck. The others all follow. They shut the door behind them.

You sigh with relief as the cacophony ceases. Everyone else's mental chaos is gone. You are alone with your thoughts—and Dr. Waldo's, as well.

Your eyes glaze over as you finally stop fighting the outside thoughts you're hearing. You discover that the thoughts are in layers, and you can separate them like the rings of an onion. The layer closest to you is Dr. Waldo's immediate thoughts. But under that, less distinct, more like a cloud, are thoughts that for him are not at the forefront of his mind. You wonder if he's even aware of all the layers. He's thinking about a project he's working on, which he wants to have Ben and Eve help him with. He's contemplating a vacation and is thinking of asking Chuck and Charlie to help him find a suitable isolated planet, one with a cottage or even space for a glamping tent by a lovely mountain lake—with no monsters. And his lunch, he is very excited about his lunch. In a layer deep beneath all of them, you discover, he is thinking about a woman. His wife. How much he misses her. You are curious, but you find yourself able to close your mind on that layer. That room—that pain—is not meant for you.

Above all this, however, foremost in Dr. Waldo's brain, he is thinking about you. He's fascinated by you. He wants to study you. He brought you into this room not because he thinks the room itself will help but because he thought it might help to have fewer voices in your head.

"It does help, thanks," you say, addressing the last thought.

Dr. Waldo's eyebrows rise up.

"Sorry," you say. "I'm not trying to read your thoughts. They're just here, in my head. It's like they're being shoved at me."

"Then you know there's nothing in this specific room that I think will help," he says.

"I know. And I know you want to study me."

"If you'd be willing. The alternative really is the magnet room across the hall. I don't know if it would work but it's the only thing I can think of. That, or you could go home and never return. It's possible, maybe even probable, that your abilities would go away if you left the Hub." He smiles. "Here, everything is possible. On our own home planets, possibility is often quite limited."

If you decide to let Dr. Waldo study you, turn to page 134.
If you choose to go to the magnet room, turn to page 160.
If you go home, turn to page 161.

"The planet with the waterfalls," you say hesitantly, looking from Chuck to Charlie and back. "Is it like a giant wall of waterfalls?" You describe in detail the scene you saw in your mind. The forest, the field, the ledge, the river, the spray, all of it.

Chuck and Charlie look at each other, then at you. "Yes," Charlie says. "That pretty well describes it. Have you ... have you been there?" He raises an eyebrow.

"No. I mean, just now. In my mind. I saw it." You pause, not knowing what to say next.

Emma shakes her head. "Well, we've established that the table is not a portal," she says.

"Have we established that?" you ask.

"What's the alternative?" Eve says.

"The alternative," Ben suggests, "is that maybe our friend here can read minds. Chuck, were you picturing that scene in your head when you were trying to get the table to move?"

Chuck blinks. "Well, yes, actually. Exactly as you just described it." His eyes narrow and he takes a step back. "Did you read my mind?"

You feel your face flushing again. "I mean, not intentionally," you say. "I wasn't trying."

"Your thoughts must have been so powerful that our friend couldn't help but read them," Emma says to Chuck. She looks at you. No, she stares at you, hard. "What am I thinking?" she says.

"I don't—" you start to say. You're pretty sure you can't read minds, but rather that the table is really a portal and you were feeling the energy—

But then you stop. Another image is forming in your mind. It's a lighthouse, but not the one you're in … or were in. This one is … you squint to see the picture in your mind's eye better.

"I'm seeing a lighthouse," you say. "The exterior is all stones. It's round and it's made up of layers of rings of stones, sort of. I mean bricks, I guess, but they're … brown. Beige. There's a tiny little entrance building attached to the base. It's also made of stones but the stones are … I guess smoother. The roof of the entrance building looks like triangles. It's black. Black tiles. The lighthouse itself isn't that tall. Maybe … well, there are some buildings nearby, one-story buildings, and it's maybe twice as high. The top part is white. A white railing around a white circular building in the center, and then another white railing on top of that around a shorter circular layer, like a cake. On top of that, a glass enclosure with the light."

You pause. In your mind's eye you turn. "There are only a few buildings here. Tidy and small. A lot of white and a lot of stone. And some grass. It's very isolated. I'm out on a … well, it's like an island but it's attached to the mainland. What's that called?"

"A promontory," Emma says under her breath. "You're at Wilson's Promontory Lighthouse in Australia."

"Is that what you were thinking about?" Eve asks Emma.

"That's exactly what I was thinking about," says Emma. She looks at you. "You can read minds."

Suddenly images start to flash in your mind from everywhere. You see a scene of a land that is very dry, vast, cracked land. You see a landscape at night, lit by two—no, three, three glowing moons. You see a room full of people who look exactly like the twins—a room full of Emmas and Rees, of Charlies and Chucks, more than you can count. You see a beach, at sunset, and you can almost feel someone holding your hand as you walk along the shore. You see a lush forest that looks prehistoric, like where dinosaurs might have lived. A word flashes into your mind, and you speak it out loud, your mouth stumbling on the strange syllables. "Plassensnares," you say. "Plassensnares?" You repeat it, a question.

"That was me," Charlie says. "Sorry about that. I was thinking of this planet we once went to—"

"No!" you say, holding your head. The images get brighter, the sounds louder, the scents more pungent. Now you're seeing computer screens and spreadsheets, labs and pipettes, people in white coats, and you realize you're starting to pick up the thoughts of everyone in the Hub, all the scientists. You notice thin threads, invisible, really, more like threads of energy, that connect each thought from your mind to a person. You can tell who is thinking which thought by the energy threads. Now there are dozens of threads, no, hundreds, and they're extending out beyond the Hub. The noise in your head is flashing louder and louder. "STOP!" you cry. "Make it stop!"

Ben puts a hand on your shoulder. "We should go see Dr. Waldo," he says.

But you just want to go home.

If you agree to see Dr. Waldo, turn to page 165.
If you decide to head home, turn to page 173.

"The magnet room," you say. "I want this to stop." You smile. "But your lunch does sound delicious."

Dr. Waldo laughs, a hearty chuckle that crinkles his eyes and shakes his body. You feel you've made the right decision. You would hate to go home and never be able to return to visit.

As soon as you step outside the door of the quiet room, the cacophony of voices invades your head again. Chuck, Charlie, Ben, Eve, Emma, and Ree are all watching you anxiously, but you walk past them without saying a word.

Turn to page 168.

"I can't do this," you tell Dr. Waldo. "It's exhausting. I just want to go home."

"All right," says Dr. Waldo. He pulls out a small dark sphere from his pocket. "You're sure? I don't know whether it will make the voices go away, but if it does, it would be best if you did not return. Unless you're prepared to try a different course of action next time you come."

"I'm sure," you say. You can hear all his doubts, and above it all you can feel his longing to study your mind. But you've made up your own mind. You want to leave.

Dr. Waldo taps at the dark sphere for a few moments, then hands it to you. "When you're ready, swipe your finger across the sphere like this," he says, waving a finger in the air above the ball. He hands it to you. "It has been a pleasure. You've given me much to think about. And I shall think about it all when you are safely away from the inside of my brain." He smiles.

"Thank you, Dr. Waldo," you say. "Please tell the others I said goodbye." You're not sure what else there is to say, so you look at the sphere in your hand. You hesitate a moment, and then swipe.

Instantaneously you find yourself outside again. The lighthouse is standing tall in front of you, giving no hint of the secrets it holds within. High in the sky, the sun sits in a cloudless sky. You close your eyes and drink in its heat on your face.

The quiet falls on you like rain. You soak it in, swim in the peace. You will never take silence for granted again.

With a final look back at the lighthouse, you put the dark sphere in your pocket and walk away.

THE END

Heck with it. Didn't someone once say that it's better to ask for forgiveness than permission?

Before anyone can stop you, you crawl into the table.

"Wait!" says Emma. "I don't think that's such a good idea—"

"You've never done anything like this before—" says Ree.

"It's dangerous—" says Eve.

"Good luck," says Chuck.

You laugh, then close your eyes. You try to think quickly, before anyone can pull you out, but no one is trying. You imagine yourself ... in a field. A field on a planet with ... two suns. A habitable planet, you quickly correct yourself. Habitable by humans. A grassy field on a habitable-by-humans planet with two suns. You imagine how it feels: it's a sunny, warm day. A few clouds in the sky. Maybe you're near a lake. A nice lake to swim in. There's no one around, you think; better not to surprise any random people and end up getting hurt. Did you mention you're in a field? Is anything happening?

You peel one eye open. The others are all standing there still, gawking at you.

You scrunch your eyes shut again. Okay, something else. You're on ... a planet—habitable—that is made of diamonds. The dirt is diamonds. There are lakes of water, surrounded by diamonds. Mountains of diamonds. Trees that ... uh ... grow from diamonds.

You sigh. That's not going to work, for sure.

Okay then. Maybe time travel. You're on Earth, but it's ... fifty years in the future. You're at your home on

Earth, but fifty years from now. You picture your house. There's a tree in the backyard, and you imagine what it might look like fifty years from now. You picture a new paint job on the house to keep it looking good. And … well, other plants are bigger, too. The cars—there's a car in the driveway that is … it's flying car.

You slowly open your eye again. Everyone is still looking at you, but they look a lot less concerned.

You try one last time. "Anywhere, portal. Just take me anywhere."

But nothing happens.

Finally, you sigh and give up. You crawl, sheepishly, out of the table. You stand and stretch.

Ree reaches over and takes your hand. "You had to try," she says. "Now. Should we go show you the rest of the Hub?"

You nod and follow the others as they show you the many wonders of the Hub. You try to create more things with the power of your mind, but it's as if the universe let you have all your ability in the first go, and there's nothing left. After a while, you head back out of the Hub, through the lighthouse, and back to the cabin. The next morning, you wonder if any of it happened at all.

THE END

Your brain is about to explode from the overstimulation. "If you think Dr. Waldo can help, then let's go," you say. Your eyes are starting to cross. You blink hard. You see the scientist across the way in the lab area, and before the others can even say anything, you are running across toward him.

"Dr. Waldo!" you call out as you approach him.

He hears his name and turns. The smile that is initially on his face falls quickly into concern when he sees you.

"What is wrong?" he says, reaching out a hand to your shoulder. "My oh my goodness, what is wrong?"

Instantly his thoughts pop to the forefront of your head, but they are images and words you don't understand. You're walking in a landscape that looks like it could be out of a Hobbit world. You're in the sky. You're on a planet where everything is faded and ephemeral. Are those ghosts?

"Everything," you say, grasping at words. "I can hear everything."

By now, Ben has caught up to you. He jumps in to explain. "Somehow, our new friend here is hearing *all* our thoughts," he explains. "Everything. Reading minds."

"Reading memories," you say. "Thoughts, memories, images ..." You look at Dr. Waldo. "You have a dessert in the refrigerator that you can't wait to eat. Some sort of ... like a chocolate mousse?"

Dr. Waldo first smiles with delight. "Oh, yes, it's an experiment, especially light and fluffy, it's not really science, but—"

"Dr. Waldo," Ben cuts in. "It sounds great. But we've got a problem here." He points to you. You have your head in your hands again and you've started to moan quietly.

"Yes, yes," says Dr. Waldo, his focus shifted to the matter at hand. "I see. Well, I see. What we need is …"

He stops speaking but you know what he's thinking. "A perfectly quiet room?" you say. "Do you have one here?" Instantly you read his thoughts again. "You think you can make one?" You doubt it but you shake your head. "Let's go to the Experimental Building, then," you say. You don't have time to wait for people to actually speak. You need action NOW.

As you race to a building in the distance, you pass a number of people and you hear all their thoughts. What you notice most of all is how much everyone doubts themselves. Two scientists standing next to each other are both wondering if the other respects them. Another scientist wonders if he has made a mistake with his calculations. Yet another is thinking maybe she should change careers. It's astonishing to you, really. You always thought everyone else had everything together. That you were the only one who was so uncertain. But now that you can hear every thought in the room, you realize you are far from alone.

As all the thoughts in the Hub drift through your mind you make your way to the Experimental Building. You race up the steps, which disappear under your feet as you walk, but you ignore it. Once you're inside the main doorway, everything is stable again.

"This way," you say, echoing Dr. Waldo's thoughts. Everyone else is trailing you but you don't need them to say anything to know where you should go. Their thoughts are like a force of nature, moving you forward.

"Left," you say when you reach a branch in the hallway. You've latched on to Dr. Waldo's mind and you hear his thoughts almost before he thinks them. He's debating between which of two rooms you should go into. One he's thinking of as the "quiet room," and the other is a "magnet room."

You reach the end of the hallway. You already know, from reading Dr. Waldo's mind, which room is which, but the placards over the rooms prove you correct.

If you choose the quiet room, turn to page 154.
If you choose the magnet room, turn to page 168.

You rush into the magnet room. Everyone else follows behind you. Ree closes the door to the room and instantly you feel something change. It's like a hum, except that it's a physical sensation rather than a sound. And somehow, the thoughts in your head … something in the room seems to be affecting them.

You turn to Dr. Waldo. "Now what?" you ask.

"Well, you see," Dr. Waldo says, "it's a hypothesis really, barely an idea. Just something that occurred to me. Whether it will work, I don't know but …"

You shake your head. Everyone's thoughts are lining up differently, like they're marching into a sort of formation inside your mind. Where there was chaos before, all the threads intermingling and weaving in and out, now the threads are straightening out. Each person's thoughts falling into a line. You can't see it, of course, but you can sense it.

"What now?" you repeat, agitated, wanting Dr. Waldo to get on with it.

"You see, our thoughts, they have magnetic properties. Not tremendous. Small. Magnetic characteristics only make up a tiny percentage of our brainwaves. But it's there," he says.

You are already nodding. Dr. Waldo notices.

"You feel it, then?" he says, his face lighting up with joy. "You can sense it?"

"Everyone's thoughts are gathering together. Like all of each person's thoughts are attracted to each other." You wave a hand. "All Chuck's thoughts are lined up over here." You wave you other hand to the other side of you. "Emma's thoughts are here. And so on."

"Yes! Yes!" says Dr. Waldo. "This is what one of our scientists has been studying! Well, then. You see, my hypothesis is your brain has become a magnet for everyone's thoughts. The normal magnetic characteristics were disrupted and now you attract all thoughts to you. I'm hoping we can just recalibrate you and ..." He looks around until he finds what looks like a football helmet, covered with wires and metal plates. "And return you to normal," he says, picking up the helmet. He directs you to a chair. "Sit," he says.

The helmet looks a little frightening. You're not the only one who thinks so. You hear Charlie think that he would never let that helmet near his head, and you're inclined to agree.

"But if I don't," you say to Charlie, ignoring the fact that he hasn't actually spoken, "then I might spend the rest of my life hearing your thoughts."

Charlie stares at you.

Ree shakes her head. "No one could stand that," she says. You know she's only half joking.

You turn to Emma. "It's interesting," you say, answering the question Emma is wondering: What it would be like to be you, hearing every thought everyone has. "But only at first. I wouldn't wish it on anyone."

Emma nods. You know she has more questions, but there's not time for that.

"Let's go," you say to Dr. Waldo. You take the helmet

from his hands and sit in the chair. "Do I just put it on?"

"It's an experiment," Dr. Waldo says, thinking the words at the same time he speaks them. "I don't really know. But yes, let's give it a try."

You put on the helmet. Even before Dr. Waldo does anything, you can feel an internal pull, like the thoughts that have been swirling inside your head are being pulled out.

Dr. Waldo steps up to a console and starts tapping away at the computer. "Stay calm," he says.

Turn to page 144.
Or turn to page 145.

You're on Earth. You've landed in the middle of a street that looks like your street. This is the tricky part, you realize. How will you know if it's your own Earth or a parallel Earth, if they look exactly the same? You take a moment to pat yourself on the back for the fact that you are, in fact, on a planet that looks like Earth, regardless of which one, and that you do seem to have returned to normal size. You ignore the fact that if you could think yourself over to another planet and regain your normal size you probably could have just made yourself normal size again back in the Hub. This is far more interesting.

You take in a breath of air. Fresh Earth air. The air in the Hub wasn't not-fresh, or anything, but now that you're outside breathing this air you decide maybe there was something synthetic about the Hub air. After all, where did that air come from? If someone in the Hub imagined there was no breathable oxygen in the Hub, would it all suddenly go away?

Not for you to worry about, though. You're here, now, on this planet Earth, and you've got to go find yourself.

You look around the block. It looks exactly the same. There's your house. And there, right out front, staring at you ... is you.

You wave and start to walk over to yourself. You cannot wait to tell yourself everything that has just happened. You know it all seems pretty implausible, but you're convinced you can convince yourself.

Suddenly you see the look on the face of your parallel self change from confusion to surprise and concern.

"It's okay!" you call out, smiling. But you realize the

other you is not looking at you anymore, but rather at the table, which you left in the middle of the street.

A large moving truck is backing up out of a driveway. The driver doesn't seem to see the table. You feel like you've gone into slow motion as you yell out "Nooooo! Stooooopppp!" but it's too late. The truck hits the table and it crumbles into dozens of pieces.

The driver of the truck doesn't even notice, but just drives away.

You look back at yourself. You can't even describe the mix of emotions on your parallel self's face.

So you take yourself aside and start slow. You explain how you found the lighthouse, then the Hub. You talk about how in the Hub everything is possible. You reassure yourself many, many times that you are, in fact, you, from a parallel Earth in another universe.

An Earth in another universe that you can't return to. Unless you find another way back.

And with that, you and your parallel self start traveling the parallel Earth. You first go to the parallel lighthouse of the one on your own Earth where you discovered the Hub, but either it is not a portal on this Earth, or it just won't open for you. The two of you then spend the rest of your lives trying to find another portal, another Hub. You never do. In the end, you and your parallel self die on the same day, within the same hour, at the age of 97.

THE END

You shake your head. "I can't," you say. "I have to go." You run toward the door that should lead back to the lighthouse, not stopping to think whether you can figure out how to get back. You step through the doorway, and it seals itself tightly behind you. Another door appears. You push it open and, gasping, fall out into the lighthouse lobby.

Silence.

You take a deep breath. You listen carefully, scanning your mind.

The only thoughts are your own.

You look back behind you and firmly shut the door.

You will never return.

You head back to your cabin. For a moment you think about turning on some music to accompany you as you walk, but instead you just enjoy the peace.

THE END

Instantly you realize your error. You should not have told yourself not to think about dinosaurs. Dinosaurs were at the back of your mind the whole time you were imagining a parallel Earth, and now, dinosaurs are right before you. You imagine that probably this is a parallel Earth ... but definitely not the right era.

One small consolation is that you managed to make yourself full size again. You know this because the two T-rexes that were—until you arrived—engaged in a battle to the death, are now staring right at you.

At least you know your portal works.

You scramble back into the table and try to imagine the Hub, but you can't focus long enough to make anything happen. The T-rexes are watching you, and you are watching them, watching with such focus this time that you don't even see when an ankylosaurs swoops in from behind you to make a deadly blow at you with its tail.

THE END

You shrug. One button is as good as the other, right? You push the blue button. Your heart skips a beat. What will happen now?

For a while, nothing happens. Next, the green button disappears, but the blue button keeps glowing, its light pulsing at the same speed as your heart. Then, you start to feel a pressure in the air—that's the best you can describe it—just a change in the atmosphere. Nothing you can see or touch but just a feeling that the air is pushing in on you from all sides. It gets stronger. Not uncomfortably so, but you hope it doesn't get much tighter.

You inhale deeply. What if the pressure continues? What if it gets so strong that you can no longer breathe?

You feel your face start to get hot, whether from the air or from the fear growing inside you. You start counting your breaths to keep you calm.

Now your ears are starting to ring. There's definitely a noise—a combination of noises. A high-pitched, very faint whine, and a low thrumming. Or are you hearing the blood as it flows through your ears?

The blue button on the wall continues to pulse. Brighter, dimmer. Brighter, dimmer. Brighter, dimmer. You start unintentionally timing your breath to the pulses. Inhale, exhale. Inhale, exhale. Inhale, exhale.

Then, it all stops.

The blue button fades away. When it's completely gone, two shapes begin to shimmer into existence on the same wall. Eventually you can tell that what has appeared is the outline to two sliding doors. One is now framed in purple, the other in orange. The colors are burning bright, inviting you to slide them open.

If you go through the purple door, turn to page 183.
If you go through the orange door, turn to page 188.

You like green. Trees are green. What could go wrong with green?

You press the green button and wait.

You feel the table start to swirl … or at least, you feel a little dizzy somehow and you assume the table is swirling. You sit on the floor to keep from falling over.

A feeling of warmth comes over you, not just physical warmth but emotional warmth. Wherever you are, you know it's a good place. Safe.

The portal shudders a bit, rumbling with a noise so low you can't hear it but rather only feel it. Your body keeps shuddering after the room has stopped. Dizzy again, you close your eyes, wondering how long this will last until you get where you're meant to be.

Finally, the room stills. You open your eyes, but then blink them again several times: It seems that the walls of the portal are disappearing. Everything inside is disintegrating before your eyes, turning into a translucent fog and then into the air itself.

Soon, there's nothing left but you.

You look around. You know this place.

You're in your own backyard, back at your house.

And, it looks like you're back to your normal size.

The universe knows. There's no place like home.

You smile and nod. Good job, universe, you think. Good job.

You head inside. It seems no time at all has passed since you left, but nonetheless you are suddenly exhausted. All you want to do is sleep. You go to your bedroom and put on your pajamas. You turn down the covers of the bed and crawl in. Almost as soon as your head hits your pillow, you are asleep. Your dreams are vivid, taking you across other planets and traveling though time.

When you wake up, it takes a minute before you remember what happened.

When you do, you immediately get dressed, and head off to find that lighthouse again.

THE END

With visions of a private beach paradise swimming in your head (almost literally), you jump into the water and start swimming up. When you reach the surface of the water you see your dream island, not too far away. You start swimming toward it, swimming more easily than you ever have. After a while you realize you don't need to pop up for air with every other stroke like you learned in swimming class. You dive back underwater and start swimming like a mermaid. You can't help but smile with joy, and even as you smile broadly, no water enters your mouth.

Quickly, you reach the shore, and you stand upright to wade the rest of the way in. The sand is pure, a bright, almost-white color. Tall coconut trees are rustling in the wind, their leaves blowing all around, exposing coconuts larger than your head. You realize you're thirsty. You find a coconut on the ground, then look around for a sharp rock to crack it open on. Your efforts are imprecise, but eventually you get the coconut open and you drink the warm, delicious liquid inside. You then gnaw a bit on the meat of the coconut. It tastes nutty and sweet, with hints of vanilla. You savor it, licking your lips and looking up at the treetops wondering how you can get more.

After that, you start to feel a little sleepy. You find a nice flat spot of beach that is shaded by trees and lie down for a nap. You fall asleep almost instantly, dreaming of shipwrecks and infinite universes. When you wake up, the sun is much lower in the sky. You are thirsty again, and hungry, so you go in search of another coconut. Along the way you find bushes with sweet ripe red berries, which you eat as well. You find another coconut and eat and drink your fill, and then you decide it's time to head back to the portal.

But when you get back to the beach, you realize you made a fatal mistake: you didn't take note of anything that would help you identify where you came ashore, and you didn't leave any markers.

You have absolutely no idea where in that vast ocean your table portal is.

You dive a few times, but you have no luck. Finally, exhausted, you come back to shore.

You realize your stomach is beginning to hurt. It keeps getting worse and worse, until you are doubled up on the beach, arms wrapped around your stomach in pain. It is only then that you remember the berries you ate. Turns out, they were poison.

In your last moments, you are lying on the beach, in a haze of pain, watching the stars fill the night sky. You fall asleep and never wake up again.

THE END

This is too crazy. Your gut tells you that appearances aren't always what they seem, and surely a wall of water that defies the laws of gravity can't be a good sign.

You slide the door shut again and go to the panel on the wall. You put your palm against the panel.

"Okay, portal," you say out loud. "Take me home, please."

Nothing happens.

"Back to the Hub, please," you say, a little more weakly.

Still, nothing. You see nothing, feel nothing, hear nothing, smell nothing, sense nothing. Nothing has shifted, and neither have you.

"PLEASE, portal," you say again. "Please take me home."

Nothing.

You go to what you have started to think of as the Captain's Chair. You sit for a while, wondering what to do next. It takes a few minutes for you to realize there's now a new door on the wall, its edges delineated by green and blue lights.

You approach the doorway without much hope. You don't want an underwater world. You don't want to be here anymore. This is no longer fun. You just want to be home.

You tap at the door, not sure how to open it, but the tapping works and it slides open.

What you see before you makes your heart sing.

You are on your street, back home on Earth. It is morning, probably early. Birds are chirping and the air smells fresh, like a new day.

You run to your house, fast as you can, like you can't get there fast enough, never looking back to see if the portal has remained or disappeared.

You are home.

THE END

The purple door is a lovely shade of purple—a little more red than blue; somewhat of a plum color. It's gorgeous, so you pick it.

As if the portal is reading your mind, the moment you're certain you want to go through the purple door, the orange door disappears and the purple door slides open.

What you see before you is a landscape so beautiful it literally makes you gasp. A short distance away off to your left, a large lake glistens invitingly, the warm sun reflecting off its deep turquoise waters. You can see people splashing in the shallow water at the shoreline, and others swimming farther out. Their laughter and excited chatter is carried to you on the gentle breeze.

Off to your right, you can see the wide front of a multi-storied castle—and as you watch, it appears that a drawbridge is being lowered over a moat in front of the structure. People are milling around the front of the castle on either side of the moat.

Farther in the distance you can see a snow-topped mountain range. Overhead, several hot-air balloons are floating aimlessly.

"You're here!" A voice calls out to you from behind you as you watch the balloons. You turn to see who here possibly could have recognized you. Your jaw drops when you see … yourself.

"Yeah, that's how we all react," the other you says. "You get used to it."

You look around now, extremely confused, and you start to realize that every person there looks exactly like you.

"Purple door, right?" the other you says. Another other you approaches.

"What?" you say. You stare at them. "What is going on?"

The second other you speaks up. "Infinite universes, right? And in a good number of them we made portals out of tables and told the universe to decide where to take us. The portals landed, and we picked from purple or orange doors."

"Hydro picked from purple or pink," says the first other you.

"So they say," says the second. They shrug. "Not everything happens in the same way in every universe."

"Hydro?" you say. That's not your name.

"Yeah, we figured out pretty quickly that we'd need different names to tell each other apart. It's hard enough that we look exactly the same."

You blink. You're almost speechless, you have so many questions.

"Hey," says the first. "Look, we get it. We were all where you are not too long ago. You'll get used to it soon enough. Anyway, come with us; you can pick out a room at the castle."

"Or make your own," says the second.

"Pick out a room?" you say. You turn back to look at your table portal. Your heart drops to your knees when you realize it's no longer there. "Did someone take my—?" you say.

"It's gone," says the first. "They all disappear."

"I'm sorry," you say. "I'm super confused. Why do I need a room here?"

The two other yous look at each other like they're trying to figure out who is going to speak. Finally the second sighs. "Here's the thing. This place is amazing—it's like the Hub, in a lot of ways."

So they know about the Hub. Of course they do, you tell yourself. They are you, from other universes, on the same life path. You shake your head. This is insane. You have so many questions.

"Just like in the Hub, here you can create anything with the power of your mind," says the first. But you can tell there's something missing from what they're telling you.

"But?" you say, prodding them.

"Almost anything," says the second, lifting a shoulder. "Except a portal. No one has figured out a way out of here."

"*Yet*," says the first. "Not yet."

Your mouth goes dry. "What?" you say, your voice raspy. "What do you mean?"

"We're all stuck here," says the first. "Us, from infinite universes, the ones who didn't pick the orange door."

"How long have you been here?" You look around. About a hundred yards away, you see a shimmering disturbance in the air, and then suddenly another you emerges from another portal. You watch as the portal sparkles and flashes then disappears behind the new arrival, who, like you, has not yet noticed. Another you sees them and goes to greet them. You watch as the newest you goes through the emotions of shock and disbelief, just as you did.

"The first of us started arriving about two weeks ago," says the second. "It's been pretty nonstop for a while. Today's been super busy."

You shake your head. "There's got to be a way home," you say.

"We're all working on it," says a third you who approached as you were talking. "You're welcome to try as well."

You shudder involuntarily. "We can create anything here, too?" you say.

"Except portals," says the third you.

You look at the castle. It looks beautiful, but you think you need some space for a bit.

You ask the others to show you where you can build your own home, and they take you to the expanding edges of this planet, or Hub, or whatever it might be. There, you create a small lake, crystal clear, and a cozy little stone cottage just for you. You create a refrigerator and pantry and fill them with all your favorite foods. You create your bedroom with a clear ceiling so that at night you will be able to watch the stars—whatever stars can be seen from wherever you are. You make a king-sized bed for yourself and cover it with the softest sheets you can possibly think up. And then, you go to sleep.

You have no idea how long you sleep, but when you wake up and go outside, a few more of you have created cottages around your lake, a reasonable distance away for privacy. Almost like they knew what would be okay with you. You walk around and notice that it does feel like more of you have arrived.

Identical yous from other universes continue to arrive for another week, after which point the number of daily arrivals quickly dwindles down to nothing. All of you start forming groups to try to figure a way back to your own Earths, but no one ever does. You live out the rest of your life on this planet of parallel yous, getting to know yourself better than you ever imagined possible.

THE END

Orange makes you think of orange juice, and you're feeling a little thirsty. You approach the orange door, and as you do, it slides to the side.

As the door opens, you gasp and your jaw drops. Before you is a literal wall of water—but the water isn't spilling into the portal. Somehow, it's being held back as if the door were still there. Is it even water? You poke a finger at the substance. Your finger goes straight into the water, but still the water stays contained. It's as if your whole world were rotated ninety degrees, and gravity is pulling from the side rather than the top.

The water is exquisitely clear. Straining your neck a bit but keeping your head out of the water, you can see some light far above, indicating that perhaps there is sky up there. Below, you see what looks like well-preserved remains of a shipwreck.

You look behind you to see if by some magic, a scuba suit and oxygen tank have appeared. They haven't.

You stick your finger into the water again, followed by your hand, your arm. You pull them back to yourself. The water stays where it was; not a drop remains when you pull your arm back through.

You stare at the wall of water for a few minutes. Why did the portal bring you here? Would it have brought you here if you couldn't explore?

Finally, almost impulsively, you poke your head through the wall of water. At first you hold your breath. But after about a minute or so your lungs scream for you to inhale. Very slowly, you start to breathe through your nose. You expect your nostrils to be filled with water;

you're prepared to pull your head back into the portal and blow the water out. But nothing happens. In fact, your lungs feel as though they're getting filled with oxygen—not just oxygen, but the cleanest oxygen you've ever breathed. No water is passing through into your body. Just air, good enough to breathe.

You exhale and watch as bubbles form in the water from your breath. You inhale again, this time with more intention, taking in a good gulp of what you're telling yourself is air. Again, no water enters your body. Somehow, you are filtering the oxygen out of the water, breathing the air but leaving the water behind.

You stick your head further out of the doorway, holding on to the sides of the door for balance. You can see perfectly clearly underwater, even more clearly than on a normal day on Earth. You see the light above you, its rays rippling in the water. You see the ship below you, but now it looks more like a regular ship and less like a wreck.

If you dive into the water and head to the surface, turn to page 179.
If you dive in and head for the ship, turn to page 190.
If you close the door and ask the portal to take you back to the Hub, turn to page 181.

Who can resist a shipwreck? Sure, it may not be all that wrecked, but if it's intact, that's even better.

You push your way through the wall of water and find yourself floating. You can see everything clearly, though sounds are muffled and seem sluggish as they move through the water around you. You've never been a great swimmer, but somehow now you're like a natural sea creature. You aim your face at the ship and wiggle your legs behind you, propelling you faster than you imagined.

In no time, you're at the ship. You grab hold of a railing and pull yourself onto the deck. You swim/walk around a bit. The ship seems to be some sort of cruise ship or ocean liner. Rows of deck chairs are lined up on the decks, looking as fresh as if they were just used earlier that day. In fact, everything looks pristine; nothing is suffering from corrosion or any sort of wear that you would expect from a ship buried at the bottom of the sea.

After swimming/walking a while, you come across two giant wooden doors, elaborately carved with the image of King Neptune on one side and an underwater paradise on the other. The matching crystal door handles are designed to look like seahorses. You pull on one to open the door, but drop it closed from surprise as you gasp at what you just saw.

You open the door again. Inside you see a scene which you are sure you must be dreaming. The room is fully lit by sparkling crystal chandeliers hanging from the ceiling. People in elegant ballgowns and tuxedos are dancing to the music from a ten-piece orchestra that is performing on the stage. Waiters are moving about with trays of champagne and sodas and fancy hors d'oeuvres.

And what's more, while the room is filled with light and music and people, one thing is decidedly absent.

Water.

Where you stand, in the doorway, just as back at your portal, again there is a wall of water being held back but seemingly nothing. Only this time, you're on the water side.

You step through into the room. Your clothes are instantly dry.

A waiter comes by and holds up a tray for you. "Canapé?" he says, offering up a platter of toast and cheese. You realize you are starving. You take a napkin and load it up with food. Another waiter comes by and offers you orange juice, which you accept as well.

You stand there, staring, until a tall woman with pure white hair, piled high with curls and jewels, wearing a long forest green gown and matching gloves, approaches you. She has a glimmer in her eye and a bright, friendly smile.

"First time?" she says.

You shake your head. "Sorry, what?"

"You're new here?" she says, sweeping her arm around to indicate the ballroom. "But you found us."

"I don't really know how I found you," you say. You're still not sure you're not dreaming.

"I imagine," she says, winking, "that you used your imagination." She stops a waiter and takes a small plate of stuffed mushrooms off his tray.

You stare at the mushrooms as if they hold answers. "I

mean, I guess?" you say. You imagined everything into existence. Did you imagine this?

"You didn't imagine this," says the woman. "But the fact that you're here tells me you used your imagination well. This ship is only open to people who have the courage to dream big dreams."

Your throat is dry. You take a sip of your orange juice.

The woman continues. "The portal you arrived in will be gone by now. But don't worry. Every elevator on this ship is actually a portal. Some go everywhere. All go somewhere. And they all come back here. So why don't you put down your food and join us on the dance floor? And then I'll give you a tour of the ship. There's much to discover," she says. "Here, everything is possible."

"Everything is possible," you say. "I've heard that before. Is this a Hub?"

The woman smiles. "It is like a Hub, but a very special kind. Not everyone gets to come here. You are very lucky." She frowns slightly, then laughs at herself. "No, not lucky. You created your own luck with your courage. Now, enough of that. There's time for you to figure it all out later. For now, let's have a dance."

You follow the woman out to the dance floor and are instantly surrounded by other people in all their finery, dancing and laughing and singing along to the songs that the orchestra is playing—songs you've never heard before, but yet somehow you know all the words.

Ten minutes later, you feel like you've known these people all your life. You look down and realize that you, too, have suddenly changed from your old clothes into a fancy ballroom outfit. You smile. You have found your own place. You know that here, you will always belong.

THE END

THE END

You have reached the end of this book. But not the end of the adventures!

Turn back to the beginning and follow a new path to see where it takes you!

THE BEGINNING

More by Pam Stucky

Middle Grade / Tween / Young Adult Sci-fi Adventure

The Balky Point Adventures
The Universes Inside the Lighthouse
The Secret of the Dark Galaxy Stone
The Planet of the Memory Thieves
The Perils of the Infinite Task

Choose Your Own Universe
(Balky Point Adventures companion books)
The Ghost Planet
Where the Universes Converge

FOR MORE INFORMATION

pamstucky.com

Thank you for reading

Made in the USA
Monee, IL
26 October 2023

45217721R00121